THE MONSTERS WALK—

The thing that wakened me was a sound from the room above. Something thumped on the floor—as if one of the horrible sculpted figures up there had taken a clumping step. I lay awake on my pillow with my heart bumping and all my senses alert. But there was no further sound, and I was just drowsing off when I heard the second noise, a familiar sliding sound like a window opening.

When the next sound came, it froze me beneath my covers—for something was tapping at my window. It was like a summons, calling me to the room of monsters which waited above. I could stand it no longer. I slipped out of bed and ran to see what was happening. I had to confront whatever it was lurking there in the dark, waiting for me. . . .

MYSTERY OF THE SCOWLING BOY was nominated for the Mystery Writers of America "Edgar" Award.

Mystery of the Scowling Boy

by Phyllis A. Whitney

A SIGNET BOOK
NEW AMERICAN LIBRARY
TIMES MIRROR

Library of Congress Catalog Card Number: 72-7272

This is an authorized reprint of a hardcover edition
published by The Westminster Press.

 SIGNET TRADEMARK REG. U.S. PAT. OFF. AND FOREIGN COUNTRIES
REGISTERED TRADEMARK—MARCA REGISTRADA
HECHO EN CHICAGO, U.S.A.

SIGNET, SIGNET CLASSICS, MENTOR, PLUME AND MERIDIAN BOOKS
are published by The New American Library, Inc.,
1301 Avenue of the Americas, New York, New York 10019

FIRST PRINTING, FEBRUARY, 1975

1 2 3 4 5 6 7 8 9

PRINTED IN THE UNITED STATES OF AMERICA

CONTENTS

–1
The Singer

I stood on the balcony outside my room at Gramp's house and stared at the snow-roofed mansion in the valley below our mountainside. It was a strange, Victorian construction, with towers and gables and dormers sticking out everywhere, giving it a distracted look. Like an old lady who doesn't know which way she wants to go and tries to face in all directions at once. It had always been an interesting house, but this December afternoon there was a real mystery about it besides.

Where it had always stood quiet, almost deserted, now the house had come to life unexpectedly, and I wanted to know more about what was going on down there.

My brother, Mike, and I had just arrived at our grandfather's house in the Pocono Mountains that morning, when Mother and Dad had driven us out from New York. They had stayed for lunch and then gone home. We always loved to visit my grandfather and grandmother in Pennsylvania, so when Mike and I found that Mother and Dad both had to be out of town over Christmas vacation, we felt good about spending two weeks in Gramp's house. Otherwise we'd have had to stay home in New York with Mrs. Abbey, our housekeeper. Besides, this would give us two Christmases, since when our parents got home we'd celebrate all over again with the presents they'd bought for us while they were away. Because they felt a little guilty, I suppose.

The woods around the house below us were thick, but from the balcony I could look right down on roofs and chimneys, almost into the heart of the house. Always before it had been still and lost in gloom. But now, even though the day was cold, a window was open at the back, and a sound of singing reached me up the mountain. I listened and thought about our stay at Gramp's.

We knew there would be wonderful skiing on the mountain behind us, and for me, I expected a rest from music. Not *my* music—other people's. What we didn't know was that instead of everything being country-quiet as usual, I was going to get involved in a really weird adventure—all because of the scowling boy.

. But before I tell you more about the house below us, you might as well understand that I'm the girl who's a square peg in a perfectly round family. Everyone in my family does something awfully well. Except me. Dad plays the violin with a symphony orchestra. Mother is a concert pianist, and they both have to travel a lot during the season. Mrs. Abbey takes care of us well, and we're used to her, so mostly that's all right. Maybe we enjoy our parents all the more because they can't always be with us.

Michael, my brother, who is thirteen and a year older than I am, has begun to grow his hair long— though only in back—and he is so good with his guitar and his songs that he has been on television a couple of times. Even Grandfather Clausen, my mother's father, while he isn't musical, is a talented wood-carver (something he learned when he was young in Norway), and some of his fine pieces are in museums around the country. He has sold them for high prices in galleries, and his work is in great demand. Gram was once a singer, but she gave it up in favor of making a home for Gramp. She is a terrific cook and loves taking care of a house. I mean, she's really gifted.

So that leaves me—Jan Sutton—outside the family circle. For the moment, that is. I have some plans to change all that. I couldn't sing, paint, write, play an instrument, dance, cook, or do anything especially well. There was just one thing that I was sure I could do, and I would have to fight to get a chance to prove it. Mother was already upset about it, and Dad was calling it all nonsense and telling me to grow up. They didn't understand that I couldn't go on being nothing in a gifted family. I was really suffering, and I had to find a way to prove myself. I wanted so terribly to be Somebody. Somebody important, famous, talented. Instead I was a real Nobody.

Gramp, who can be quite poetic at times, says I'm the bud on the rosebush, and it just isn't possible to know what sort of bloom I'll turn into. He keeps telling me there's lots of time yet. But I look at all the blooming talent around me, and I don't believe it. There *was* one thing I could do. If only they'd give me a chance. It was not something as easy as painting or playing a guitar, which you can do right inside your own home. This talent requires outside opportunities and help. But I could feel inside myself that it was the thing I could really be good at, if only I had the chance.

Anyway, here we were at Gramp's mountain house, with Christmas and New Year's ahead. I could let down for a little while and not sense Dad and Mom watching to see when I was going to bloom—yet squelching me when I tried.

Gramp's house has always fascinated me. It is set a little way up the steep side of the mountain, perched on a ledge of rock, with an almost vertical drop toward the valley below. The way Norwegian houses are often built, Gram says, since she has been to Norway on visits with Gramp. It is a sort of Swiss chalet type of building, with brown and white decorations and a long balcony across the front. A steeply slanting roof hangs over on all sides and shields the house from storms. The rooms inside are all pine-paneled downstairs, and painted cream color upstairs.

I especially like my bedroom. It's at one side, with a small balcony where I can stand and view the mountain and the countryside. Gram says Gustav Clausen (Gramp) had to have lots of balconies because he remembers the long winter nights in Norway. The Norwegians value the sun and arrange to get out in it whenever possible.

The mountain the house perches on is so high and long that you can see it standing up from the countryside for miles around. The slope behind the house is covered with a thick evergreen forest, and only a few houses have been built on that side. Around on the far slope are the base lodge and the ski area, which we can get to easily.

Closer, directly below at valley level, is the old Victorian house I've been telling you about. As I understand it from things Gram has said in the past, an old man who was an invalid lived there with a granddaughter who took care of him. There was a maid and a cook, because he was rich. But until now nothing ever seemed to happen down there. The house huddled in its gloomy woods and peered out from among the trees through all its windows and towers. I hardly ever saw anyone but the servants coming and going, and once in a while the granddaughter walking on the paths around the house. She usually dressed in black and seemed a somber figure.

Now, though, there was a difference. I had seen a boy about my age run around the house, and once I saw a tall, slim woman in yellow pants come outdoors

—someone I'd never seen before. And now there was the singing. On a record, of course. I knew the song because I had it on a recording at home. The voice was the voice of my favorite movie actress, Alanna Graham. She was singing "Lilac Grove" from her last picture, and I sort of hummed the tune along with the player. I couldn't really sing, but I went along with the tune inside my head and murmured the words softly. I could remember Alanna Graham in the picture, dancing among those lilac bushes and drawing the children along with her. She could sing and dance, but she was mainly an actress, and I'd been devoted to her for a long time. Because I had decided that this was what I wanted to be—an actress.

It was true that I'd been in only one school play, and then in a very small part, which I hadn't done awfully well. But I loved to think about other people and imagine what they were like inside. I knew I could *be* other people, if only I had the chance. In my room at home I tried to read poetry aloud, and parts from plays that I brought home from the library. Sometimes I made faces at myself in the mirror and tried to mimic the manners of other people close to me. I played at showing rage and joy and despair—until I got to giggling.

I didn't understand why Dad called all this nonsense, and Mother insisted that I was too young to think about acting. I wanted terribly to go to a school for young actors. I wanted to be a child actor right away. And my family—even Mike—all thought I was completely crazy.

The voice from the house below lifted on the clear air—and then broke off suddenly. It wasn't a mechanical break, and for the first time I realized something strange. The record wasn't like mine at home. It was the same song, the same voice, but now there was no accompaniment—no orchestra, no sound of piano and violin. I leaned on the balcony, gripping the rail with my mittened hands. That hadn't been a record at all! A real woman was singing down in that house, and she was singing with Alanna Graham's voice!

As I stood there staring down the mountainside, the woman in yellow pants came to the window and closed it, shutting in all sounds. I couldn't see her very well, but even from this distance, she looked familiar. It was possible. She could be Alanna Graham!

I turned back to my room feeling terribly excited. I was supposed to be up here unpacking, and I finished in a hurry. Then I ran toward the stairs and was in time to meet Mike coming out of his room. My brother, Michael, has brown hair and brown eyes, just as I do, though I'm the one who wears hair to the shoulders. He's taller and broader, and he's also much better-looking. Which doesn't seem fair. I keep reminding myself that I'm an unopened bud and that I may be a beauty later on, but in the meantime, Michael has the looks.

"Did you hear the singing?" I asked, running after him on the narrow stairs that dip steeply down along one wall. Norwegian stairs, Gram says.

Mike reached the bottom step and turned around to look up at me vaguely. "What singing?"

If I didn't know how smart he is, sometimes I'd think my brother was awfully dumb. I expect it's because he lives off in some sort of dreamworld a lot of the time and doesn't know what's going on around him. You mustn't think his mind's always on guitars, though. He's also interested in anything that hums, or buzzes, or chugs. I mean engines, motors, and the insides of such. A nice gummed-up motor will really turn him on. Which means that he'll be off in a fog and not know what's going on around him for days at a time. Dad says he'll probably turn out to be a scientist or an inventor.

"There's a singer living in the house down the hill,"
I told him.

I could almost see him pulling himself back to real-
ity, as his eyes began to focus.

"She was singing 'Lilac Grove,'" I ran on, "and she
sounded like—well, anyway, I think she must be
somebody tops. Let's go ask Gram who's living in that
house."

Gram was in the big airy kitchen, a room that was
really my favorite in the whole house. The walls were
pine and there were interesting wooden cupboards and
shelves with ornaments from the Scandinavian countries, besides a few carvings Gramp had done especially for her. I particularly liked one little Norse war-
rior with a helmet decorated with horns, and carrying
a spear and shield. He looked wonderfully fierce, and
Gram said he was the guardian of the kitchen.

Gram herself never looked like a housewife or a
cook. She was tall and rather dignified, with her head
held high and her gray hair wrapped around her head
in braids. I'd never in my life seen her in a housedress
or an apron. She usually wore a skirt and a colorful
Norwegian sweater with the sleeves pushed up.

She was busy now making some remarkable honey-
and-bran cookies from a recipe of her own. My mouth
started to water just looking at the pan lined with rows
of brown dough chunks, as she popped the cookie
sheet into the oven. I have seen women put cookies in
the oven before, but they never do it with Gram's air.
She was almost dramatic about it, as though she were
performing on a stage, instead of in a kitchen. I hadn't
had a chance yet to tell Gram about my ambition, and
I wondered if she might be more sympathetic than the
rest of the family.

"Who's living in the house down the hill?" I asked
her. "There seem to be more people there now."

She flung the oven door shut with a little slam and

flickered up her hand as though she wished the cookies luck. It was an eye-level oven and she didn't have to bend over and straighten up. She gave the green sleeves of her sweater a tug on each arm and walked over to the sink. Her motions were all very sure and graceful, and I found myself wondering if she ever missed the life she had given up so that she could stay with Gramp. She wasn't ignoring my question—just thinking about it. Mike looked longingly through the glass door of the oven at the cookies. He was also able to think about food.

"Yes, I know," Gram said at last, with a little nod of her braid-decorated head. "Apparently the old man's other granddaughter has come home, bringing her son with her."

"What's the old man's name?" I asked.

"Burton Oliver," Gram told me. "We've never met him, and we hardly ever see him unless someone wheels him out onto a porch or a balcony. Everything is usually very quiet down there."

The name Burton Oliver didn't help me, but that didn't mean anything. Alanna Graham might not be her real name at all.

"Do you know who the granddaughter is?" I pressed Gram.

"I believe her name is Mrs. Anna Nelson, and the boys's name is Steven. But she has another name too. I was talking to someone at the post office about the new arrivals just yesterday. They always know everything at the post office. It seems that she's an actress from the films, named Alanna Graham."

I gasped because until that moment I'd found it hard to believe in the voice I'd heard. This little part of the Pocono Mountains was a long way from Hollywood, and it didn't seem that I could be lucky enough to have Alanna Graham for a neighbor. All at once a great stirring and plotting began to start at the back of my mind. How could I get to meet her? How—how?

"That reminds me," Gram said. "There's a talk show due on television right now, and I read in the paper yesterday that Alanna Graham was going to be on. I thought I'd like to watch, since she's our neighbor for a while. It must have been taped earlier, of course, because she's down the hill now. Is either of you interested?"

Mike wasn't especially, but he came along into the living room for want of anything better to do, and of course I practically ran for the television set. Gram turned it on and set the dial for the right channel. The program was already on, and the screen showed Alanna Graham's lovely face in a close-up.

She was so beautiful. Yet beautiful in a strange way, because if you added up her features separately, each had some slight flaw. Her mouth was too big, and her eyes set almost too far apart. Her nose went up at the tip, and her chin was square in a way that didn't match the rest of her soft, oval face. Yet none of this mattered. She flashed her famous smile at the man who was interviewing her, and all you saw was her grace and beauty. She was matchless, really, and I had a terrific crush on her. I'd have given anything to look like her, be like her, and by comparison she made me feel young and awkward and awfully plain. And a little scared too. Scared of myself. Because I knew I wasn't going to leave her alone down there in that big house. Somehow—somehow, I was going to meet Alanna Graham. I was going to talk to her. Because maybe she could help me. I fixed my eyes on the television screen and took them away for only a moment to frown at Mike, who was squeaking his chair.

Alanna had very black hair which she wore piled in a fanciful way on top of her head. I'd have thought it would slither down when she moved, because it looked precarious, but I suppose it was lacquered into place.

This was color television, so I could see the pale green on her eyelids and the cinnamon-red lipstick. A little strand of jade beads was caught in her hair, and she wore a long, patterned robe that was a rich wine color, with blobs of big yellow flowers all over it. She looked very dramatic—the way an actress ought to look. When she answered questions her voice was resonant and throaty and you knew it must be a good singing voice. At the moment when we tuned in she was talking with great enthusiasm about her son.

"Steven is a brilliant boy," she said with an emphatic wave of her fingers. "I'm sure he'll be a distinguished writer or philosopher when he grows up. He is always reading, and his teachers think he is very gifted."

"In what way is he gifted?" the interviewer asked.

"Oh—" Alanna Graham seemed at a loss for a moment, and she fluttered her beautiful hands, so that I wondered suddenly if she was making some of this up about Steven. "Oh—he likes to write and paint. I'm afraid I don't always understand the things he does. They're often quite gloomy and full of death and disaster."

That sounded real enough, but she still looked flustered for some reason, as though the subject of Steven disturbed her, and the interviewer began to talk about something else.

"I understand you're going to be staying with your grandfather?" he asked. "Doesn't he own a Victorian mansion out in the country?"

She was willing enough to talk about the old house in which she had grown up. Her parents had died when she was young and her grandparents had raised her.

"Wasn't there some tragedy?" the interviewer asked. "I seem to remember—"

"It was an accident," Alanna Graham said quickly, and went on to tell of her grandfather, who had pro-

duced noted sculpture in his day, before his health
failed and he couldn't work anymore.

Her words made the house in the valley seem more
real, and I could imagine the pain of that old man who
lived on there after he had to give up doing the work he
loved. I was happy to hear Alanna talking, happy to
get this real-life view of her—if it was real life. Sometimes she seemed a little stiff as she talked, as though
she was acting. Not acting with ease and grace as she
did on the screen, but as though she talked quickly to
conceal some uneasiness that lingered underneath her
words and made her manner a little false. I wondered
if she could be nervous about the interview and trying
to conceal the fact. Surely an actress would be at ease
at a time like this. Or would she? An actress, I sensed,
was used to being someone else. She had other people's
words put into her mouth. Maybe it was hard to get
out in front of millions of people on television and just
be yourself. I could imagine what it might be like,
and I felt a little prickly, as though I was out there in
front of a microphone. Oh, I *could* be an actress!

But she managed to talk fluently until the interviewer tried to bring her husband into the conversation. It had been in the papers that Alanna Graham
had separated from her husband, Bruce Nelson.
There had been some scandal about that—he was taking drugs or something. But when his name was
brought in, she closed her mouth and shook her head
and wouldn't talk at all. The interviewer had an awkward few minutes getting her onto another subject.

Gram had to go out to the kitchen to look at her
cookies, and the program came to an end shortly after.
I was left with a spell upon me. The spell of that glam-
orous, successful world in which Alanna Graham received such tremendous applause. How wonderful to
be like that. Not to have people wondering to themselves because, in a talented family, you had no talent

at all. Having people admire and applaud you and think you were wonderful. But dreaming wouldn't get me into Alanna's shoes.

"Come for a walk," I said to Mike. "I'd like to get a closer look at that house down there. Maybe we can catch a glimpse of Alanna."

"What good will that do you?" Mike said, but he didn't ask where we were going. He knew. There was just one place where we could have a really good view of the house. We put on our outdoor things and followed the snow-packed road as it curved above a rocky cliff that cupped in the big house below. Mike began to tease me a little on the way. When he isn't being dreamy and faraway, his face can take on a mischievous look, and I could tell he was seeing through my interest in getting a look at the house. He knew I didn't mean to stop there.

"When do you plan to attack?" he asked.

I didn't let his words bother me. "I'm not sure. But I have to meet her, Mike. I just have to meet Alanna Graham."

"Why?" he asked me bluntly.

I couldn't tell him that. I hadn't really worked it out for myself yet. After all—what could she do for me, even if I met her? I only knew I had to try. She was everything I wanted to be.

We came to a place where a stand of hemlocks grew, their branches drooping thickly around a hollow center—just like a green cave. We'd found the place the very first time we had visited Gramp, when we were much smaller.

Snow was deep at the side of the road, but we stamped it down with our boots and crawled between green branches to get into that central hollow. Because the hollow was protected by the trees, the snow wasn't deep in there. On the outside rim, a rampart of rock rose from the hillside and we could climb to the ledge it made and look over, down through an opening in the trees, practically into the rear windows of the big house. Mike boosted me up, and I pulled him after me. Then we leaned our arms on the rocky wall in front of us and gazed down on all those old towers and gables of the house below.

—2

The Scowling Boy

"Look!" Mike said and nudged me.

I found the window he meant at once because it was the only one that wasn't blank and empty. The shutters were open and a boy was leaning in the space behind the pane. He had seen us up there above him, and he scowled at us in a way that showed angry disapproval of our spying. Mike grinned at him and waved, but the boy—Steven, undoubtedly—only scowled more furiously. He reached up to unlatch the window and flung it open. Then he leaned out and shouted something at us, but the wind snatched the words away, and we couldn't hear what he said.

I grabbed Mike and we slid down from our ledge. There was space beneath the hemlock branches at one side to peer out without being seen, so we moved our station, watching the house from a hidden angle. Not far from Steven's window was a small balcony, and evidently his shouting had been heard because the balcony door opened and Alanna Graham came through. She stood there, very slim and tall in her yellow pants and gray sweater, until Steven came and joined her. They both searched the mountain with their eyes, but of course they couldn't see us now. Steven continued to scowl, and Alanna didn't look pleased. In fact, she looked worried and a little frightened, and I was sorry about that. After a moment they gave up and went in out of the cold. Watching them go, I felt discouraged.

I hadn't made a very good start, getting both Alanna and her son annoyed with us, and I only hoped he hadn't had a really good look at us before we got out of sight. That is, so he wouldn't recognize us again. At least I'd had a close enough look at her by this time to know without any doubt that the woman in the house below really was Alanna Graham. My longing to meet her, talk to her, grew stronger than ever.

"Had enough?" Mike asked me.

I shook my head. "I want to meet her," I said doggedly. "I think I'll go down and try the front way."

"You mean just walk up to the front door?"

"Why shouldn't I?"

"What will you say if you meet someone who asks what you want?"

"I could say I'd like her autograph, couldn't I?"

Mike smoothed his frowzled brown hair with a despairing hand. "Where will that get you? What if she just gives it to you and sends you away?"

I glanced at him curiously. "What do you think I want of her?"

"Probably to have her tell you she thinks you're going to be a famous actress," he said, going right to the heart of the matter in his usual way.

We had started toward Gramp's house, and I walked along beside him trying to be remote and dignified. He had touched on what I hadn't even admitted to myself, since it sounded silly put into words. Because my idea of meeting her wasn't very sensible, I was trying to cloud it over without pinning it down in any clear light. Put flatly that way by Mike, there wasn't anything I could get from Alanna. So I wasn't going to put it that way. I preferred to keep the whole idea cloudy and vague and let matters develop as they happened. Even though I didn't want to be clear about it—couldn't be clear about it—there was still something that might come out of a meeting with Alanna.

"You don't have to come with me," I told Mike stiffly.

"That's good, because I'm not. Coming with you, I mean. If you want to make yourself look foolish, go ahead. I thought maybe Steven might be somebody worth knowing, since there aren't any other kids around here our age. But he looks bad-tempered, so you can have him, if you like."

I didn't try to answer. I didn't want Steven either— just his mother. We parted when Mike went up the drive to Gramp's house, and I continued along the road that wound down the mountain. The air was cold, but the sun was bright, and patches of snow were beginning to melt along the way.

As I walked I thought about the view I'd just had of Alanna. I'd had the same feeling about her that I'd sensed briefly on the television program—that she was not a woman who was altogether easy in her mind. Looking up the hillside just now, she had seemed worried, just as she had at times on the program. There was something wrong in Alanna Graham's life, and I wondered what it was. I didn't want anything to be wrong for her. She was beautiful and successful, and she had everything—except, maybe, a husband. I tried to imagine how happy and contented I would be if I were in her place, but this time I couldn't quite make it inside Alanna's skin. I didn't know her well enough, I realized.

I had seen her many times playing various roles, but what the real woman was like who lived behind all those different faces was hard to figure out. Not that the faces were so very different. Alanna Graham had what the movie people called "an image." She always played lovely, noble roles in which she was sweet and good and generous. She was always sacrificing herself to help other people, and you knew she was good clear through. That was one reason why I was brave enough to think of meeting her. I hoped she would be like that in real life, too, and would be kind to me. Still, I couldn't be sure.

I was down on the level now, with the mountain rising behind me, and I walked more quickly as I approached the driveway that led to Burton Oliver's house. I'd passed it many times in Gramp's car, so I knew right where it opened off the road through a stand of pines. You couldn't see the house from the road because the driveway twisted and lost itself among the trees. There was no gate where it started—just a postbox with the name OLIVER on it.

When I reached the box I stopped and stood beside it, trying to figure out what I wanted to do. The only excuse I could think of was the one I'd given Mike—to go in and ask for Alanna's autograph. If I could get her to talk to me in a friendly way, perhaps I would think of something else and find out how to get better acquainted with her. I wished her son, Steven, had seemed more friendly. That scowl he wore offered nothing promising.

But there was no use standing there stirring around in my own rather muddled thoughts. I braced myself and started boldly up the driveway, walking at a good, fast pace. The first turn of the winding way cut me off from the main road and set me in the heart of a thick forest of pine trees. Without meaning to, my steps slowed. Dark, shaggy pine tops rose above me, cutting off the sun. Long shadows of late afternoon cast tree-trunk shapes across my path in dark stretches that made me feel uneasy. There was a wind whispering through treetops but no other sound in the forest, so it seemed as though something unseen was rushing by overhead. I began to think that there couldn't be any

house set deep in the woods, and that I would get lost
if I kept on following the curving drive.

I had to shake myself and tell myself this was silly.
Because of course a driveway led somewhere, and I
knew the house was in there. After another turn I
heard sounds a little way ahead—a scampering and
thudding, then a shout. There was someone close by.
I hurried around the next bend and came to a halt at
the edge of the trees in order to watch the scene before
me.

Beside the driveway a clearing had opened and a dog
and a boy were playing there. The boy was Steven Nelson, Alanna's son. The dog was a Doberman—big and
black and strong. Steven called him Thor as he flung a
stick across the clearing for the dog to retrieve. Both
boy and dog were so engrossed in what they were doing
that neither saw me on the edge of the drive, and I had a
better opportunity to study Steven at close range.

He wore dark blue ski pants and a lighter blue
sweater. His head was bare and his thick curly hair
was black like his mother's. He had very dark blue
eyes, a thin, handsome face, and he was fairly tall.
When he moved, however, it was with a limp, and I
wondered if he had hurt himself or if he'd been born
that way. Then I saw his boot on the right foot and
noted that it was built up to accommodate a shortness
in his right leg.

He tried to run after the black dog, and even as I
watched, he stumbled and fell, stretching himself full
length on the snow. The dog darted over to him, thinking this was part of the game, but the boy thrust him
angrily aside and got awkwardly to his feet. Then he
did a strange thing. An apple tree with gnarled
branches grew at one side of the clearing, and when
Steven was on his feet, he flung himself toward it,
climbed up into a niche in the thick trunk, and then
crawled out on a branch. All his movements were

angry, defiant—as though he was bent on proving something to someone who didn't believe him.

I think I understood. His bad leg had made him fall, defeated him when he tried to run, and now he was proving himself to himself by doing something he could do—climb a tree. The black dog, Thor, dashed around the tree, barking and jumping up toward his master. I wished I could fade out of sight on the driveway. I wanted to step back among the trees, return the way I had come, but it wasn't possible.

The dog saw me first and increased his barking, his forelegs stiffening into a defiant stance as he threatened me. Steven saw me next. He sat up on the branch he straddled and looked across at me with the same angry scowl I had seen on his face earlier.

"What do you want?" he said.

I was afraid of the dog, and I began to back away, not trying to answer the boy.

Steven shouted at Thor. "Stop it!" he cried. "Stay!" and the dog lowered his barking to a growl and stayed where he was.

"Who are you?" Steven said when I didn't answer his first question.

Apparently the dog was going to mind him, and a little of my courage began to return.

"I'm Jan Sutton, from the Clausen house up the mountain," I said. "My brother, Mike, and I are visiting our grandparents for the holidays."

"So what are you doing here?"

"Just following the drive," I said. "I suppose it goes to the house."

"Was it you up the hill a little while ago?" he demanded. "Spying on us?"

There was no use trying to fool him. "We were interested in the new people at the house."

"We don't like spying," Steven said, swinging his

legs up around a branch. "And we're not new people. We belong here."

I had the feeling that he was mainly angry with me because I'd seen his display of emotion when he had fallen and then climbed the tree.

"I'm sorry," I said. "We didn't mean to spy. It's just that Alanna Graham is my very favorite actress and I wanted to make sure she was the one who lived in that house."

"So what if she does?"

"I wish I could meet her, that's all. It must be wonderful to be the son of somebody famous."

"Not so wonderful," he said.

I wondered why I had thought him handsome a few moments before. His dark blue eyes were bright with an angry light, his brows drew down in that thick scowl, while his mouth—rather a big mouth like his mother's—was a straight, grim line. He was worse than a watchdog, really, and I could see that he meant to keep me away from his mother if he could. Just to be contrary, I supposed, and to prove himself in command.

"I—I wondered if she would let me have her autograph," I said hesitantly.

He snorted at me from his tree branch. "Don't you think she has other things to do than sign her name for everyone who comes along? That's square anyway—collecting autographs. What can you do with them?"

As a matter of fact, I had rather a good autograph collection at home. Mother and Dad knew lots of famous people in the musical world, and sometimes they came to our house. They never minded signing my book. But I couldn't explain all this to Steven. There wasn't anything to do for the moment except to give up in defeat and go away. Perhaps I'd try the driveway another time when it might be empty and I could get as far as the house without being stopped. I turned and walked away without saying good-by.

Behind me Thor growled again, but he didn't come after me, nor did Steven. I walked back toward the road, retracing my way through the dark trees. They didn't seem any less menacing after my meeting with the boy who lived at the big house.

Nevertheless, as I walked along, something happened in my thinking about him. In spite of his scowls and the way he had behaved, I couldn't help feeling sorry for him because I'd had a glimpse of the way his bad leg made him suffer. And I was admiring too—because he had proved, however angrily, that he could overcome the handicap in some ways. I found myself wishing he would be more friendly, because I had the feeling that he might be worth knowing, once I could get past all those guards he seemed to wear to hold people off. That was one of the troubles with me. I could never stay mad very long.

It was a relief to reach the open road after the closed-in forest, and I was glad to feel the afternoon sun slanting down on me, relieving the darkness of the trees.

Did Steven have any friends, I wondered, tucked away as he was in that house? Probably he didn't live there for long at a time, since his mother must have to be out on the West Coast working for a movie company. I wondered if this was just a visit to his great-grand-father.

When I reached Gramp's, I went around to the side of the house to see whom I could find. Gramp was out in his workshop next to the garage, and Joe Reed, the handyman, was with him. Gramp usually had a handy-man who helped with the heavy work around the house and grounds, and there was a good place for him to live in a partitioned-off part of the garage, where Gramp had put in living quarters. There was a kitchen at one end of a small living room, and a tiny bathroom with a shower in it.

Mike and I had met a long string of handymen who had worked for the family since we'd been coming to visit Gramp, and they were apt to be strays of one sort or another. They worked for a while—some of them hard and some poorly—and then wandered on to another job somewhere else. Joe Reed seemed a bit different. He appeared willing to take more responsibility than most. But he was on the gloomy side and he held everyone off from being friendly. He was probably in his early forties and he had a hollow-eyed, hungry look about him. Gramp said he thought Joe might have been ill for a while and wasn't very strong yet. But he had seemed anxious to work, and since Gramp didn't have anyone at the moment he had taken Joe Reed on.

I wanted to tell Gramp about Steven Nelson, and Joe just stood there listening while I talked, making me feel a little uncomfortable. I explained about wanting to get Alanna Graham's autograph.

"I'd love to meet her, and I thought this might be a good idea," I said.

Gramp nodded sympathetically. He hardly ever criticized anything Mike and I wanted to do, and he was always interested. Gramp was tall, with broad shoulders and no stoop. His hair was a rather shaggy gray and he had light blue eyes with crinkle lines at the corners that came from laughing a lot. He had grown up in Bergen, Norway, and had come as a young man to this country, where he'd met Gram.

"And did you succeed in this purpose?" he asked me.

I shook my head. "I met her son, Steven, and he didn't want me around. He said she wouldn't be bothered giving autographs."

"Perhaps it would have been better to call up on the

phone and talk to her yourself," Gramp said. "Then she would probably have told you to come over and Steven wouldn't have stopped you."

That would have been a sensible approach, but it didn't suit me. I wanted to *meet* Alanna. I didn't want her to give me her autograph quickly and send me away. And the farther I got from my goal, the more important it began to seem to me. Somehow I had to see her before I went back to New York. Mother and Dad would have to listen if someone like Alanna thought I should be encouraged. There! It was out in the open in my own mind—the foolish thing I hoped for from Alanna Graham. The very thing Mike had accused me of. Though was it so foolish? If she would just listen to me . . .

"You're plotting something," Gramp said, smiling a little. "Well, I won't interfere. Though I hope you won't become a nuisance to our neighbors down the hill."

"Alanna Graham always gives autographs," Joe Reed said unexpectedly. "She's supposed to be very gracious about it."

He spoke in his usual gloomy, rather unfriendly tone, and both Gramp and I stared at him. It was as though a stick of wood had started to speak. He stared back at us, undisturbed.

"There's a piece about her in that old stack of magazines you gave me," he told Gramp. "I read it there."

I pounced on that. "Could I have the magazine?" I asked.

"Sure. Come along and I'll give it to you."

I followed him to the door of his living quarters and looked in. The room looked the same as always. There was a daybed, and a table with a couple of chairs. A fat-bellied black stove burned wood for heat, and the kitchen at the back was very clean and neat. Joe had made no changes in the room from the last time I'd seen it, but he kept it in a more orderly state than some of Gramp's handymen had.

He fished the magazine out of a stack and brought it to me. I flicked through the pages until Alanna's face looked out at me, and at the sight of it I couldn't help sighing. It was usually necessary to be beautiful to go on the stage or be in the movies, I thought sadly. And I was never going to be beautiful. But still, there were actresses who had succeeded anyway. And with make-up and all that, they could make anybody look better nowadays.

"Her eyes are set too far apart," Joe Reed said critically.

I gave him a quick look and wondered if he had interpreted my sigh correctly and was trying to encourage me. But he didn't look encouraging. In fact, he went off about his own work without another look at me or the magazine, and I carried it back to Gramp.

He stopped me before I went into the house. "Your grandmother isn't feeling well," he told me. "I'm worried about her lately. Help her all you can, will you, Jan?"

"Of course," I said.

"When would you and Mike like to go skiing?"

"As soon as possible," I said eagerly.

He nodded. "First thing in the morning then. You can tell Mike."

I went inside the house and found Gram lying on the living room sofa. I hated to see her not feeling well, and I asked if there was anything I could do. She smiled at me a bit faintly and shook her head. I went upstairs to my room and out onto the balcony before I took off my things. From this distance the house below looked as quiet and empty as though it were unoccupied. Steven was nowhere in sight, and neither was Alanna.

I would still find a way to meet her. And it wouldn't

be by calling her on the telephone. Perhaps I'd take this magazine along and ask her to sign her name across the picture. When I'd taken off my ski pants and parka I sat down in my room to read the magazine. The piece was the usual souped-up sort of thing they like to do in fan magazines, and I didn't learn much from it I didn't already know.

There were pictures of her home in California, and a picture of Alanna and Steven, with Steven looking as though he didn't want to have his picture taken. I couldn't find any reference to the house in Pennsylvania or to Alanna's grandfather. Probably the writer didn't even know they existed. There was some rather messy stuff about her broken marriage and how beautiful women so often married the wrong man. I suspected that Alanna and Steven must have hated the article, but that was the trouble if you were famous—you couldn't prevent anyone who wanted to from writing about you.

Later that night, after dinner, when I'd come upstairs to go to bed, I put my coat on over my pajamas and stepped out onto the balcony for one last look at the Oliver house before I went to bed. There were lights on down there—quite a few lights. I knew which room was Steven's because I'd seen him in the window, and there was a light there behind closed blinds. I wondered again why he had looked so angry with us and wondered why he had put himself out to be unfriendly when I'd come upon him in the woods. I might have liked to have him as a friend, because he seemed rather a brave boy, but it was clear that he hadn't wanted to make friends with me. It was clear that he would stand in the way of my meeting Alanna if he could.

Down in our own yard something moved, and I saw a shadowy figure near the side of Gramp's house. A man stood there quietly, looking down at the lighted windows of the house below. I wondered if it was Gramp. To find out, I tiptoed across my room and opened the door to the hall, listening. From downstairs I could hear the deep rumble of his voice as he talked to Gram, and I knew he was indoors.

I went back to my balcony and watched the figure for a little while. It was Joe Reed, and I wondered what he was thinking as he stared at that big old house where a rich and famous woman lived. For the first time I really wondered about Joe and where he had come from. And why a man like that had been interested in the piece in the magazine about Alanna Graham. She lived in a faraway world from his. He was out of step with life, while Alanna was right in step with it—having everything.

It was cold on the balcony, under the bright, icy stars, so I blew out a frosty breath and ran back inside to curl up beneath the warm blankets on my bed. Dad was up in Montreal tonight, and Mother was out in Chicago. Both were a long way off. And mostly when they were off they couldn't even be together. I tried to imagine them being in those strange places, but all I could see in my imagination was theaters. Theaters were theaters anywhere. Some were better than others, but they were all made with stages and orchestra pits and rows of seats for the audience.

Thinking of those hollow theaters where my parents were playing made me feel lonely, even with my grandfather and grandmother downstairs. Was this the way Steven Nelson felt too when his mother was away on location and he had to stay home alone? Probably we had a lot in common, if only I could get past that angry wall of resistance he built up around himself.

Thinking made me sleepy, and before I knew it I had dozed off and gone fast asleep.

—3

Meeting on the Slopes

The first thing I knew, morning light was streaming through the balcony door. I came wide awake, remembering where I was, and that this morning we would go skiing.

Gramp was wonderful on skis, and Gram was pretty good too. It was Gramp who had taught us to ski on small skis when we were little and had insisted that we learn the right things and know what we were doing. So Mike and I were pretty good at it now, though we didn't get to ski nearly enough.

I slid out of bed and managed to get the bathroom on the first try. Then I dressed and followed my nose downstairs. Mike wasn't up yet, but Gram seemed to be feeling a little better and she was in the kitchen making pancakes. There was a wonderful smell of bacon in the air that made me hungry just to sniff it.

Gram's silvery hair was braided as smoothly as ever around her head, and she looked very dignified and in command of the kitchen.

"You can set the table, Jan," she told me briskly, and I hurried to carry plates and silverware into the cheerful, pine-paneled dining room. There was a yellow cloth on the table, and yellow napkins that matched the sunlight, and Gram had set a green bowl filled with evergreen clippings and some red holly berries in the middle of the table.

33

The bright room seemed far removed from the sort of things that had haunted the night. I tried not to think of a boy who scowled too much, or of a beautiful, famous woman who seemed anxious and afraid of something. This morning was for fun, so I put all that away from me. Or tried to, at least. Somehow it lingered at the back of my thoughts, casting a shadow. One day had gone and I had not yet met Alanna Graham.

Gramp appeared next, his eyes a pale, clear blue in the early morning light, and Mike came down a bit sleepily a little later. We all had a cheerful breakfast together and talked about the ski slopes and other things.

Gram said, "On Sundays we ask Joe Reed in for a good dinner, but the rest of the time he likes to keep to himself out in the garage, and he gets his own meals."

"Doesn't he have any family?" I asked.

Gramp shrugged. "He told me a little about himself when he came, but he doesn't talk much and we don't ask. It's better that way. He knows he can come to us if there's any trouble, but we don't expect anything of him in the way of confidences."

I thought of the lone figure I had seen out on the terrace the night before, watching the Oliver house. "He doesn't seem very friendly," I said.

Gramp was uncritical. "That's his business, as long as he does his work."

Gram said she didn't feel like skiing with us today, so after breakfast I went upstairs and got into my ski pants and parka and regular boots. My ski boots were on trees and I carried them and my skis out to Gramp's car, which he was loading. Mike joined us there and helped Gramp put all our skis in the rack on top of the car. While they were fastening the skis securely, I walked over to the terrace wall and looked down at the big house. Right away I saw something interesting.

Alanna Graham was outside alone in the yard beside her car. She was dressed in ski clothes, and she too was securing skis on top of her car. My heart began to thump with growing excitement. If Alanna was going to the same ski area, there might be a chance of running into her over there. In fact, I'd make it my business to find her, if she was there.

In a few minutes we drove off, waving to Gram. There had been no snow for a few days and the road around the mountain was clear. Of course the snow-making machines on the slopes would have been at work all night, and a crew would have groomed the surface, so there would be no lack of snow there.

I always enjoyed the drive around the mountain and up to the base lodge. The road wound through pine and spruce and hemlock, and there were only a few houses, tucked into the woods here and there. The air was wonderfully clear and different from the city. I wished that it were possible for my mother and father to give up what they were doing and move out here like Gramp and Gram. But of course that wasn't possible. They had to be in the city because of their work. So I'd just better enjoy this while I could.

When we pulled into the parking lot behind the base lodge, the first thing I saw was Alanna Graham walking toward the lodge, wearing her ski boots and carrying skis over one shoulder. She had come here to ski, and if she was going to be up there on the slopes, I'd find her—I'd make some kind of beginning. It was especially good that she was alone and that Steven Nelson would have no chance to get in my way.

She looked lovely in chocolate-brown ski pants and a parka to match, and she walked long-legged—not exactly gracefully, because you can't be graceful in ski boots, but managing pretty well. She disappeared around the side of the building while we were still getting into our boots and taking our skis down from the rack. By the time we had our skis on and had started toward the ski lift she was nowhere in sight. There was a choice of several different lifts—T-bars, J-bars, a poma lift, as well as a rope tow—but we were going to take the chair lift up to Devil's Drop. That was the name of the steepest run, and Mike and I were good enough to come down the most expert runs by this time, thanks to Gramp's stern training. I could only hope that Alanna was taking the same run, and that we'd meet her somewhere along the way.

This was a weekday and fairly early, so we had no wait to get a chair. It was a triple chair, so we could all go up at the same time. I sat in the middle, with Gramp on the tower side, and Mike on the outside. Gramp brought the blue metal safety bar down in front of us, and I held on to my ski poles with one hand and the bar with the other. We tilted our skis to clear the mound of snow just ahead of the chair and went rattling and swinging up into the aid.

I always loved the ride to the top. I could still remember when I was smaller and could go only to the halfway station, but now I could go to the top of the lift and come down all the way. Our shadows, flung across clean white snow, followed us up the clear space beneath the blue lift towers, climbing the mountain as we climbed. The thin spears of our skis made parallel black lines on the snow.

As we rose high in the air, we could see a few other skiers coming down the various runs that were cut between stands of evergreen trees. Up near the top, the growth grew scrubby and not very thick, but farther down the mountain there was still heavily wooded growth, with the trails winding between.

All the way up I kept a sharp eye out for Alanna, to see if I could glimpse her chocolate-brown figure coming down any of the runs. But there were others in brown and I couldn't be sure.

When we reached the top we tilted our skis again so they wouldn't hook on the edge of the platform, and left the chair to snowplow along to the ramp where we could schuss down to level ground.

In case you don't ski and wonder what I'm talking about, to snowplow is to turn your front ski tips toward each other and push along in a V, using your ski poles. It's good for going slow along a level, or for slowing yourself if you're going too fast. When you schuss, you just go straight ahead with your skis parallel. Usually you schuss on a gentle slope, because you'd go too fast down the fall line. And that's another thing—the fall line is an imaginary line straight down the mountain. Mostly you christy back and forth across it to keep your speed under control.

There was more or less level ground up above the top of the runs. There I looked about for Alanna right away. She was nowhere in sight. Three different runs opened up from this area, and she might have gone down any one of them, since she would probably use the chair lift. If I went down with Gramp and Mike, I could imagine us circling round and round and never meeting Alanna at all.

"I think I'll stay up here this time and wait till you come back," I told Gramp.

His ski outfit was all gray, and he wore a red-and-gray knitted stocking cap on his head. Under it his light blue eyes looked at me thoughtfully.

"You have something in mind?" he said.

I nodded. "I do have something in mind." I didn't say what, but I tried to make my expression say, Please don't ask. If I had to explain about Alanna, Mike might want to stay with me to see what happened, and I wanted to meet her alone. I didn't really know what I was going to say, and I didn't want anyone listening to me and criticizing.

Gramp nodded back gravely. "Very well, important affairs must come first. You will wait for us here and come down with us on the next run."

"What's up?" Mike asked curiously.

"We do not ask young ladies about their whims," Gramp said. "You can follow me down the slope, Michael."

Mike poled after him, with a look over his shoulder at me. As I watched them start down Devil's Drop, I felt a little regretful, wanting to do what they were doing. But I knew I had to wait and see if Alanna came back up the chair lift.

I went over near the platform, where I could watch the chairs swing upward toward the top, and I watched each load as it approached the platform. More skiers were arriving now, but it still wasn't crowded as on the weekends. I saw her well ahead of time. She had a chair to herself, and the long shadows of her skis moved along the ground far below as her chair climbed to the platform. Then she skied gracefully down the ramp.

I had a moment of hesitation, uncertain about just going up and speaking to her. Mother said asking for autographs could be nervy and a nuisance and should be done only at the right time. I wasn't at all sure that the top of a lift was the right place or time, and besides, now that my chance had come I felt a little in awe of her. I'd met other famous people—but no one quite like Alanna Graham, who was my idol. I didn't feel like tearing after her the way some awful autograph hunters might have done. I stood watching dumbly as she moved away from me—until I knew I was about to lose her. Then I made up my mind.

When she started toward the top of the runs, I skated after her. Skating is something you can do on skis. It's just the way it sounds, and you push off with each foot when you want to work up speed.

"Excuse me!" I called.

She stopped poling and looked around in surprise.

"I hope you don't mind," I said. "You—you're Alanna Graham, aren't you?"

In her pictures she's always kind and gentle and thoughtful and sensitive about others. She always makes family films. But of course I didn't know what she was like in person, and for just an instant I thought she looked displeased. I was afraid she was going to turn her back and push herself away from me without answering. Then she seemed to realize that I was only a young girl, and obviously wasn't going to snatch at her or be a nuisance.

"Yes, I am," she said, still surprised. Probably she didn't expect to be recognized way out there on a Pennsylvania ski slope.

"I know you live in the house down at the foot of the mountain," I went on a bit breathlessly. "My brother and I are visiting our grandparents in the house just above yours. The Clausens. I—I've loved seeing your pictures. I always go when there's one playing, and I wondered if—that is, if you'd mind giving me your autograph?" I wasn't doing it a bit well, and I floundered as if I were blowing my way through a snowdrift.

She stared at me almost suspiciously, but at last her face crinkled into a smile that made her look beautiful and not unfriendly.

"Of course I don't mind," she said.

I remembered then to tell her who my parents were so she'd feel better about talking to me. She smiled again and said she thought she had met my mother once a year or so ago.

"I'll be happy to give you an autograph," she said.

"The trouble is, I don't have a pen or a piece of paper with me."

Of course I didn't have my autograph book either— it was back in New York. And neither did I have any paper or a pen. We stared at each other blankly for a moment, and then she laughed. It was a beautiful sound. She had stopped being suspicious of me.

"I tell you what," she went on. "Perhaps you and your brother would like to come to tea at my house this afternoon? Say about four? Then I can give you my autograph properly. I have a son and I think he might enjoy some company his own age, so we'd like having you."

This was better than anything I'd hoped for. This was everything at once. I returned her smile and wagged my head in a vigorous nod of acceptance.

"I'm sure we'd love to," I said, answering hastily for Mike. "Thank you very much, Mrs.—uh—Miss Graham."

Her laugh was light and gay—as though she'd never been one to be worried or suspicious. "Just call me Alanna. Everyone does. You've really made me very happy. I know Steven will be excited."

I doubted that he would be, and I wondered if I ought to tell her I had already met him. But the circumstances had been so unfavorable that I didn't want to dampen her own enthusiasm by telling her about them.

I snowplowed along with her to the top of Devil's Drop and watched her go down, graceful as she turned her body in a christy. Then I went back to the top of the chair lift and waited for Gramp and Mike to come up again. I felt happy and triumphant, yet a little anxious at the same time. What happened next would depend on me. I didn't mean to accept that autograph and run. I wanted to get really acquainted with her and somehow to get her interested in me. It wasn't going to be easy to blurt out my ambition and ask her to help me. In fact, thinking about it, it seemed next to impossible. Yet it had to be done somehow. I had to find a way.

Gramp and Mike weren't long in appearing, and the moment the two of them came down the ramp I began to tell them about the invitation.

Mike was not altogether pleased. "Tea? You mean I've got to dress up?"

"It won't hurt you," I said. "This is awfully important to me. And it will be fun to get inside that old house and see what it's like. You can get to meet Steven and—"

"I don't think Steven is anxious to meet us," Mike said.

But I wasn't going to think about that. If his mother brought us in as guests, he'd surely have to stop scowling. And he couldn't block my way into the house when I was there at his mother's invitation.

But I was dreaming again, and Gramp was watching me thoughtfully. "This is a very kind gesture," he said. "I did not know you were acquainted with this lady."

"I wasn't," I admitted. "I asked for her autograph, and when I told her we were neighbors she invited us for tea."

Gramp nodded with a twinkle in his eyes. "I see. And this pleases you?"

"Yes, of course. She's absolutely my favorite movie actress. So I think it's wonderful."

Mike had started off toward Devil's Drop, and Gramp and I hurried after him. I'm sure Gramp guessed that I was planning something, but he didn't ask any more questions.

When we reached the top of the run, I got Mike to let me follow Gramp down the slope. I like to ski behind him because he's so good that he knows all the best maneuvers, and all you have to do is follow him and do as he does. He never tries anything too hard when he's skiing with us.

He started down ahead of us, his skis hissing in the snow as he took the turns, and I was after him in a moment. There's nothing quite like going down a ski slope on a beautiful cold morning with the sun bright and a blue sky overhead. All the world seems spread out below you—though of course you don't have any time for view-watching while you're moving. In fact, it's best not even to look straight down. You deal with each problem of the slope as it comes up and you'd better be paying attention.

The moguls weren't very high because the machines had cut them down recently and they hadn't had time to build up again. Moguls are the packed mounds of snow that are caused by skiers carving their turns and throwing more and more snow up until it builds into a hillock. Moguls used to bother me when I was learning, because they were something you had to go around, but now I could use them to help me turn.

The wind rushed into my face, and I could feel my hair blowing back—I never wear a cap unless it's extra cold. I used my poles to help me turn and I got so excited and began to feel so skillful that I forgot to watch hard enough. My ski tip caught, and in seconds I was sliding along on my back with my feet in the air. One ski binding released, and it was a good thing it was fastened to my boot by a thong or it would have gone flying and perhaps hit someone on the way down. That's why safety straps are required. Then you don't lose your skis when the bindings release, as they are supposed to do in a fall.

Mike was behind me. He shouted, "On your left!" so I scrambled out of his way. He edged his skis, managed to slide to a stop just below, and called back to see if I was hurt.

I laughed and waved one foot in the air, so he went

on down the slope. When I'd fastened my ski back on, I got up and followed him. But a little more cautiously. Falls are a part of skiing and you can't always help them. The slopes are different every day, sometimes even from hour to hour when there's melting and freezing, and there's never any being certain, even on familiar runs.

Gramp and Mike were waiting for me when I schussed out on the level near the foot of the slopes, and we did the circuit several more times. At last we took off our skis, and still wearing our boots, we clumped into the big A-frame building, where we sat at a bare wooden table and drank steaming hot chocolate out of thick mugs. Chocolate never tastes so good as when you've been out in the cold skiing, I always think.

"What did you want with Alanna Graham anyway?" Mike asked me.

"Just her autograph," I told him. "For my collection at home." I didn't explain any further because I didn't want Mike to think any more about what I was up to. But I knew Gramp suspected something.

He laughed with a deep rumble and nodded at me, smiling. "You are the member of the family who never gives up. I wish you luck in this enterprise." And he toasted me with his mug of chocolate.

After that, it seemed a long time till four that afternoon when we could go down to the big house. When Gram heard about the invitation, she made sure that Mike and I had freshly pressed clothes, and that we were well combed and neat. She made it clear that she wanted us to honor ourselves and our parents and grandparents as well. When she was through getting us ready she was tired and had to lie down again. I hated to see her not feeling well, and I was sorry to make extra trouble.

When the time came, we walked down the snowy

road to the Oliver driveway. With Mike along, the trees didn't seem so gloomy and forbidding, but I still felt uneasy, just the same. There was no telling how this visit was going to turn out.

This time we didn't come upon any thin, handsome boy around the turns in the path, and there was no black dog named Thor waiting for us. Before long the house loomed ahead. It seemed to sit strangely there among the trees, peering at us out of all its many windows. There was no one about, and the quiet of the snowy area off the driveway was intense. It was as though no one expected us—as though perhaps no one lived there and our coming was all a mistake.

But I knew that wasn't possible, so we walked up the steps to an entry porch and confronted a door set with heavy brass hinges and presenting a big brass door knocker in the shape of a lion's head. The lion snarled and stared at us out of fierce eyes. It wasn't a very welcoming sight, and somehow I didn't want to touch it. Mike, however, was undisturbed by such imaginings. He lifted the brass ring around the lion's neck and brought it down resoundingly against metal.

We could hear the echo go ringing away inside the house, but for a few moments absolutely nothing happened.

—4

The Room of Monsters

When the door opened, it did so almost secretly and very quietly. It was pulled ajar a crack, and then all movement stopped. The crack was dark, but presumably someone was staring suspiciously out at us. There seemed to be no one to address, so Mike and I were silent, even Mike waiting uneasily now.

Slowly the crack widened to let us view a woman who stood in the opening staring at us. She was a tall woman, and quite thin, so that her long face had a gaunt look. Her red hair was drawn back from a central part and wound into a thick coil at the back of her head. She wore a black dress that was a little longer than current styles and her legs were encased in black stockings. When my mother wore sheer black stockings, I thought she looked rather elegant. This woman had no elegance about her, but she wasn't dowdy either. Her clothes seemed to suit her, and she suited the house. The word "Victorian" came again into my mind.

This time I managed to find my tongue, since Mike was staring in surprise at the dark figure and wasn't going to speak.

"We're Jan and Michael Sutton," I said. "Miss Graham invited us for tea."

A long thin arm flung the door wide and beckoned

us inside. "I'm Mrs. Price," she said. "We were expecting you."

She certainly hadn't behaved as though she was expecting anyone, but at least we had been invited to come inside. The great, square hallway was dimly lighted and completely walled in some dark, lustrous wood that gave off a dim shine in the subdued overhead lighting. There were two or three pieces of heavy, dark furniture, some tall-backed chairs that looked as though they belonged in an ancient castle, and two large chests of drawers. On one of these was set a handsome Greek jar with a fat neck and open mouth. I was to remember that jar later. Most of the light came from a wheel-like chandelier hung over the exact center of the hall.

"You can take off your coats and hang them there," Mrs. Price said, indicating a wooden clothes rack against one wall.

As I obeyed, I looked about the great hall. At the back a little more light came through windows above the curving stairs that marched upward into further darkness. I began to feel more than ever in awe of all this dignified gloom that seemed anything but welcoming. I wished Alanna or even young Steven would come down those stairs. But there was no one to greet us except the forbidding Mrs. Price. Was she the housekeeper, I wondered, or some member of the family? Hadn't Gram said something about a granddaughter who took care of the old man, Burton Oliver?

Our guide moved ahead of us toward a door on the right and flung it open. "In here," she said curtly.

The hall was cold, but across the doorsill was a hearth with a lighted fire. I hurried through the massive doorway and Mike came after me. This room, I knew instinctively, would be called the drawing room. It was much too grand to be a mere living room. It was vast and high-ceilinged and also furnished with a good deal of heavy, dark furniture. Since the room was so big, pieces of the furniture were grouped here and there like the furniture in a hotel lobby. Scores of people could have been lost in it. There were wall hangings and large framed paintings, though there wasn't enough light to tell what they were all about.

"You can sit down here," said Mrs. Price, sounding a little like the keeper of the prison.

She gestured toward the one oasis of light and warmth in the room, and I moved toward the fire eagerly, trying not to be sorry I'd come. The wide fireplace had a marble mantel and its hearth glowed with blazing logs. Drawn up in a half circle in front of it was a long couch of flowered velvet and several large armchairs. There were also two welcome floor lamps and a table lamp, all throwing a soft glow that banished the rest of the room to shadow. Distant windows let in very little light. I sat hesitantly down on the edge of the couch and held out my hands to the warming blaze, while Mike flung himself into a chair.

"What a creepy place!" he muttered.

I could only agree. No wonder Steven Nelson scowled a lot if he lived in a place like this. With all the vast room lost in shadow behind me, I had to suppress the feeling that if I looked around quickly, I might see some horrid shape slinking away into black haze.

The worst of all this was that it made me feel hopeless about getting to know Alanna Graham. How could anyone ever be easy and friendly in such an atmosphere?

But it was a little different when Alanna came into the room. She opened the door and rushed in with a little laugh of apology, holding out a hand to me and then to Mike, bringing a light of her own.

"I'm sorry to be late in welcoming you," she said breathlessly. "There was a crisis upstairs and I was delayed. Hello, Jan. And this is Mike, isn't it? I'm so glad you've come. Steven will be down shortly. I hope Cousin Daphne took care of you all right."

Her words seemed to rush out too eagerly, as though she was trying to cover something up. Because I couldn't take my eyes off her, I noticed everything about Alanna. This afternoon she wore black velvet pants and a long-sleeved white silk blouse. About her waist was knotted a wide scarf of red Scottish plaid that hung in a fringe down one leg. Her black hair was caught back with an old-fashioned tortoise-shell clasp at the nape of her neck and hung free down her back. She wore only a little lipstick by way of makeup. But what arrested my attention most of all were her dark eyes, set in the white oval of her face. There was a shine about them and the lashes looked wet. Alanna Graham had been crying, and she was now nervously trying to hide that fact.

She began to ask me brightly about my parents and where they were, and she seemed sorry that we wouldn't all be together over the Christmas holidays. She asked how I'd enjoyed skiing on the mountain, and mentioned that she meant to take Steven out skiing tomorrow morning.

"He's exceptionally good for his age," she said.

I must have looked a little blank, because she ran on, still talking a little too much and hastily explaining.

"Steven has a bad leg, but we've had a special built-up ski boot made for him, and it works very well. Perhaps we'll see you out on the slopes tomorrow morning.

"Perhaps," I said, filing away the information that Alanna would be out skiing tomorrow.

All the while she talked I knew that something was troubling her deeply and that she was using most of her effort to hold back more tears. This made it all the harder for me. With Alanna lost in her own troubles, she wasn't going to have much time for mine.

Steven came into the room shortly after, and while he looked rather sullen and unwelcoming, at least he wasn't scowling. He said hello to me and was introduced to Mike. But mainly he watched his mother, and I had the feeling that he was angry with her. Whether he had caused her tears or not I didn't know, but at least he knew she had been crying and he was watching her somewhat resentfully. It was clear that there was an uncomfortable feeling between them.

A little later a maid brought in a large tea tray and set it on the coffee table before the fire. Mrs. Price returned to the room to join us, which didn't add much in the way of gaiety. Alanna sat next to me on the long couch, while Mrs. Price sat at the other end, her smooth red hair shining in the firelight, all the rest of her a dull, drab black. She was older than Alanna—probably well into her forties. She paid little attention to Steven or Mike and me but talked to Alanna as though we weren't there.

"Grandfather Burton had a very bad night," she said. "He was restless and irritable and I had a hard time getting him to sleep. He kept trying to send me away, but of course I wouldn't go."

"Perhaps you should leave him alone more," Alanna said. "I know you work very hard to keep him comfortable, but I can remember that Grandfather always liked to spend a great deal of time alone. Anyway, we mustn't bother about all this, Cousin Daphne, when we have company."

Cousin Daphne sniffed as though she didn't consider the company very important and accepted a cup of tea from Alanna. Then cups of hot chocolate were poured from a pitcher for Steven, Mike, and me, and we were encouraged to help ourselves to gingerbread.

"Tell me about yourselves," Alanna said. "What do

you like to do at home? Do you like living in New York?"

I supposed we did. Anyway, it was where we lived. But questions like that always leave me a little blank, and Mike couldn't seem to find any answers either.

"My brother plays the guitar," I offered. "Maybe you saw him on television last month. He played one of his own songs."

Mike squirmed and made a face at me, but Alanna pounced with delight on a possible topic for conversation. She pressed Mike with questions and he got interested and began to answer them. But nobody talked about me, and I didn't know how to say anything about the thing that interested me most. When there was a pause I managed a question for Alanna.

"Did you live in this house when you were a little girl?"

She nodded. "I did indeed. It seems like an old friend to me when I come back to it now. I know that others sometimes think it's gloomy and old-fashioned, but I've always loved it."

"It's spooky," Steven said. "I'll bet the third floor is haunted."

"Only by memories," Alanna said quickly. "You mustn't say things like that. When I was a child I had a playroom on the third floor and I was up there a great deal, high among the treetops where you can feel the wind blowing."

Steven managed a small scowl. "I hate that room where Great-grandfather keeps all those old sculptures."

Cousin Daphne made a muttering sound deep in her throat, as though she agreed with him.

"Grandfather's sculpturing was the most important thing in his life at one time," Alanna explained. "That room was his studio and he had a special skylight built into the ceiling."

"Spooky," Steven repeated. "It's also the room where Great-grandmother—"

His mother spoke sharply. "That's enough, Steven. There are some things we don't talk about in front of guests."

There was a moment of sharp antagonism between them, and I knew they were dueling with each other. Finally Alanna sighed and spoke to him more gently.

"When you've finished your chocolate, perhaps you'd like to take Mike and Jan upstairs and get out some of your games. You hardly ever have anyone around to play games with."

Steven was clearly not interested in playing with us. He sat in a chair by himself, with one leg drawn up under him, so that the built-up shoe was tucked out of sight.

"What games do you have?" I asked, hoping to draw him out a little.

He shrugged. "Oh, Monopoly and checkers and other things. The usual games."

Alanna looked uncomfortable and a little sad. I could guess that she had wanted very much to have this tea party turn out right so that Steven would find new friends. But she was perhaps too upset about some trouble of her own and Steven was resisting us, though I didn't know why, and regarding his mother critically besides. Mostly other kids seemed to accept Mike and me without any trouble and we never had any difficulty making friends, but Steven was different, and I knew he was resisting his mother's efforts.

When the last piece of gingerbread had been eaten by Mike, Steven suddenly made a suggestion of his own.

"If you've finished eating, I'll show you my great-grandfather's sculptures," he said.

I looked questioningly at Alanna and saw her startled expression. She wasn't altogether pleased, and I could sense that Steven was teasing her in some way, perhaps daring her to say no.

"I don't know if they'd be interested—" she began, and Cousin Daphne burst into words for a change.

"Of course they won't be interested. Those sculptures are over the heads of most adults, and I don't think they're a bit suitable for—"

"Wouldn't you like to see them?" Steven broke in, asking me directly.

Anything would be better than sitting there and wrangling. "We'd like it very much," I told him, knowing Mike would come along willingly enough, since he liked anything that had action in it.

"Then go ahead, dear," Alanna said to her son. "But don't play any tricks. Do you understand?"

That wasn't very reassuring, but Steven smiled at her and his smile was surprisingly sweet and calming— except that I suspected it was a bit treacherous. "I won't," he promised.

We went out into the hall, and at once the black dog, Thor, got up from his place near the door and trotted over to Steven, who leaned to pat him on the shoulder. Since we were inside the house and apparently accepted by the family, Thor didn't object to Mike and me—he just didn't pay any attention to us. Mike likes dogs, though, so he went quietly about making friends with Thor, and the dog seemed to accept him after a few minutes.

The stairs went up past mounting windows and opened onto the second floor. We climbed them quickly and Thor came with us.

"My room's down this hall," Steven said, but he didn't stop. The third floor was our goal.

Here the stairs narrowed, the dark banister drawing close and curving around as it climbed toward the top floor. There were no windows up here, just a long corridor with doors opening off each side. Dim lights burned at intervals in wall brackets, so it was gloomy, but not wholly dark.

On the floor below, some doors had stood open, but up here they were all closed and the dark paneling had a rather forbidding look. As we passed one door, Steven reached out and touched the wood.

"That's my favorite room," he said.

He didn't offer to show it to us, or to tell us why, but went right on to another room a door away. Thor stopped beside him and made a low, strange growl in his throat. Steven tried the knob, found the door locked, and reached for a key which hung on a hook nearby. That seemed strange. Why lock a door and then hang the key beside it for anyone to use? Mike noticed the same thing and he put our thought into a question.

"Why do you lock the door if the key is kept right there?"

Steven's good-looking face was pale in the dim light of the hall, as he grinned at us with a flash of white teeth.

"Great-grandfather wants it that way. He wants them all locked in, so they can't get out and do any damage."

I gasped softly. That was somehow an awful thing to say. This upper floor that Steven had said was haunted gave me a creepy feeling, and I didn't know if I wanted to go into a room full of objects that might come to life and try to get out. But Mike was practical as usual.

"You're putting us on," he said. "Doesn't that come under the heading of tricks?"

Steven's grin didn't change. "You can ask Great-grandfather, if you like. But now that you're here, come on in."

For once we didn't need to switch on lights. The sun had reached this side of the house and it was pouring in two long outside windows and through a skylight overhead, throwing the shadows of the window frames and patches of late afternoon sunlight across the floor. All about us loomed tall figures, some of them shrouded in sheets that shone in the bright light. There was a workbench with sculpturing tools neatly laid out on it, as for the hand of a sculptor who might return at any moment. The air seemed stale and shut in, with the cold smell of old stone, unheated and turned a little damp. Thor brushed against me and I was suddenly aware that his coat seemed to bristle, as though he didn't like this room any better than I did.

Briskly Steven began to flip off some of the coverings, revealing the figures beneath. I wished he had left them on.

Burton Oliver had not chosen to create cheerful, normal figures of men and women. These were men and women of a sort, but all were tormented in some way, and all were rather ghastly.

I found myself standing beside a larger-than-life-size lady in a long, flowing robe. Her head was tilted sideways and she wore on her face a sly, wicked look. In one uplifted hand she grasped a small demon in the shape of a baby dragon. She was not afraid of the demon, but it was clearly afraid of her, and its cheeks were puffed out with the effort it was making to escape her grasping hand. I stepped quickly away from the lady, and was nudged in the shoulder by the sword of a knight who was fighting some imaginary enemy. I leaped back with a cry and found Steven laughing at me. Unexpectedly, however, he was kind.

"Don't mind," he said. "I felt the same way the first time I came into this room. When you stay in it all by yourself the first time, you begin to feel as though all the imaginary monsters are chasing you. Great-grandfather had quite an imagination. Quiet, Thor." He reached out a hand to soothe the dog.

Mike was not moved by such imaginings. He was genuinely interested in the figures and the artistry that had gone into sculpting them. He exclaimed over the expressions of the faces, the skillful modeling of hands, the graceful fall of folds of cloth.

Steven left him exclaiming and went to one of the windows that looked out upon treetops. He unlocked the latch and flung it upward so that cold winter air blew into the room and cleared away the stale, damp smell. He spoke without turning around.

"This is the window my great-grandmother fell from when she died," he said.

Again I found that I had gasped softly. Steven liked to shock, as I could see. He was a little like some of the figures around us in a sense—he grasped people rather cruelly to see them writhe. I knew that in a moment he was going to tell us more—tell us something hideous that I didn't want to hear—so I started for the door without waiting for any more.

"I don't like this room. I'm going downstairs," I said.

Mike was surprised, and he looked after me without moving. Steven slammed the window shut and moved toward the door.

"If your sister's scared," he said to Mike, "then we'd better go. Come on, Thor."

He wasn't being kind anymore. He was making fun of me. I didn't care. I went into the hall, blinking in an effort to see in the dim light after the brightness of that room. Even the hall seemed spooky to me now. I could well believe that something haunted it. Perhaps only memories, as Alanna had said, but they would not be happy memories.

Mike left his study of the sculptures reluctantly and followed us out of the room. Thor bounded ahead as though glad to get out of that place. Steven locked the door again and hung the key on its hook. I could easily believe that something in that room might try to get out.

As we walked toward the stairs, the house seemed to pull itself in around us, as though the very shadows were filled with creatures that pulsed and breathed and waited to get at us.

I shook myself angrily. All this was pure imagination and I didn't have to put up with it. Those stone and marble figures in the sculpture room were only that—stone and marble—however eerily they had been formed. Still, I was the first to reach the stairs and start down.

"Wait!" Steven said behind me. "Don't go down yet. I'd like you to meet my great-grandfather."

I didn't know whether I wanted to meet the old man who had created all those horrid figures, but I came reluctantly back up the stairs. Steven went toward a door at the opposite end of the hall and knocked on it. Cousin Daphne came to the door and opened it, but Steven didn't pay any attention to her. He looked past her into the room.

"Great-grandfather? I've brought some visitors upstairs. They're staying at the Clausens' up the hill. Would you like to meet them?"

There was an answer I couldn't hear from inside the room, and then Steven turned toward us. "Come in. He wants to meet you."

—5

The Puzzles Mount

The room we stepped into was filled with more gloom because the sun didn't strike this side of the house, and draperies were already drawn against the coming night. It was a large, high-ceilinged room, with heavy chests of drawers against the walls, as well as armchairs and a leather couch. But the heart of the room was the bed.

It was a huge four-poster topped with a canopy, and with curtains at one end. Propped against pillows, the thin figure of Burton Oliver was almost lost in shadow. I was mainly aware of bright, penetrating eyes peering out of a gaunt, sharp-chinned face.

Cousin Daphne set herself to block us from coming in, and her red hair seemed the only bright spot of color in the room.

"He's tired, Steven," she said. "I don't want him to get all stirred up again."

The old man in the bed spoke over her voice and his tone was surprisingly strong. "Come in, come in," he said testily. "Let me have a look at you. But leave that dog outside."

Steven pushed Mike and me toward the bed, so we were forced to approach whether we wanted to or not. When I stood close to the bed, the same thin hand that had waved us in reached out and grasped me by the wrist, pulled me nearer.

"Hello, little girl," he said. "What's your name?"

"I'm Jan Sutton," I told him weakly. I kept thinking that this was the man who had dreamed up all those strange sculptures, and I was a little afraid of him.

"And this is Mike," Steven said, giving my brother a shove so that he stood beside me close to the bed.

I could see the old man better now. He seemed very old, and the hollows and planes of his face formed shadows and highlights that made it seem like a mask. I wanted to twist my hand from his grasp and run away. But he still had some of his sculptor's strength and he held me where I was.

"I've just been showing them your sculptures," Steven went on, and I knew he was trying to stir something up deliberately.

But old Mr. Oliver seemed pleased. "And how do you feel about them?" he asked me.

While I was trying to think of something to say, Mike answered for me and I was glad of it. "I was wondering how you managed to carve that marble. I don't know much about it, I guess. But everything looks so real. Imaginary, but real."

The old man smiled at him. "Good boy. You're observant, I see. Imaginary, but real—that's a good description."

"Jan was wondering why you want them locked up when the key hangs right outside the door," Steven said.

This was the last thing I wanted to ask, but the old man regarded his great-grandson thoughtfully for a moment and then looked at me.

"*They* can't get it if it's hung outside," he said, his voice turning quavery. "Don't you think it's possible to create something out of your imagination that can get away from you and come to life on its own?"

"Now, now, Grandfather," Daphne Price said. "You

know the doctor feels you shouldn't let yourself think such thoughts."

"But I do think them. When I was making all those figures—those men and women and creatures—I used to wonder if they had a life of their own when I turned my back. I just feel that it's safer to keep them locked in. After your Grandmother Margaret died—"

"Hush. You mustn't disturb yourself," Cousin Daphne said.

I found myself shivering in the gloomy bedroom. I wanted to get away from there, get away from this house. Or at least back downstairs to Alanna Graham, who didn't have anything spooky about her.

"I think we have to go home now," I said to Mike.

Mr. Oliver let go of my wrist. "Well, come back and see me another time. I like young people. Steven doesn't come in to see me often enough. Young people keep you young, you know." His laughter was a thin cackle and it didn't make me feel any easier.

I said good-by to him politely and headed for the door as soon as I could. Mike came after me, followed by Steven. Thor waited for us in the hall. Steven was laughing at me slyly.

"The old man's spooky too, isn't he? Remember what I said about the third floor? It's haunted all right. How would you like to live in this house? I'll be glad when we go back to California. Then maybe my mother won't worry so much."

"What is it that worries her?" I asked.

We were in the hall, and Steven's look moved from me to the door of the old man's room behind us. I turned my head and saw that Daphne Price had come to stand in the doorway and was listening.

Steven shrugged and started toward the stairs. "I don't know," he said.

There was a look of intense distrust on the woman's

face and she didn't move from the doorway until we reached the head of the stairs.

"Where is Mr. Price?" I asked Steven.

He grinned slyly. "He left her a long time ago, and she came to live with Great-grandfather Burton. Which is a good thing, I suppose, because she has nurse's training. But she complains all the time about being overworked, so I don't know if she appreciates being given a home."

I felt more uncomfortable than ever as we went downstairs. Steven seemed a strange boy. You couldn't get close to him and really be friends. Nor did he seem to have any affection for his great-grandfather. Yet I still had the feeling that a lot of what Steven seemed to be was a cover-up—a hiding of feelings that he didn't want to reveal. I wondered if there was any key that would unlock him as he had unlocked the door to the room on the third floor.

As we reached the foot of the stairs, the front door opened and a man came into the house. He was tall and good-looking in an angular way, with a face rather like a hawk's, and sharp gray eyes set beneath dark brows. He came into the hall, taking off his coat and hat and hanging them up. Ahead of me on the stairs Steven came to a halt and did not move. Thor growled. The man seemed not to see us there. He strode toward the drawing room, where Alanna probably waited, and disappeared through the door.

Steven let out a long-held breath. "That's Harry Mercer," he said in a voice so low that I barely caught the words. "He's my mother's business manager from California."

I stepped past Mike, closer to Steven on the stairs. "You don't like him, do you?"

"I hate him," Steven said. "He'd like to get Mother to divorce my father and marry him. But even if I can't see my father anymore—" he ran down the stairs without finishing his words and went toward the drawing room, beckoning Mike and me to come with him.

We were in time to see Mr. Mercer cross the wide room and kiss Alanna on the cheek. She seemed very glad to see him, and she clung to him for a moment.

"Oh, I'm glad you've come, Harry! I've just had another of those phone calls and they frighten me. You know I had them when you were here before too. The voice always whispers and I can't tell if it's a man or a woman."

Harry Mercer put an arm about her shoulders protectively, and I could feel Steven's inner rage as he stood beside me. Alanna, seeing us there in the doorway, flushed as though she hadn't meant us to hear her words.

Steven walked into the room. "What phone call?" he demanded.

Alanna's bright flush stayed in her cheeks. "Oh, it's nothing that concerns you, dear."

Steven scowled at her, and Harry Mercer spoke soothingly.

"Just a business matter," he said.

Steven continued to glower and I wondered about him. So much about Steven seemed mysterious. I never knew what he was thinking or what he intended. And I wondered what lay behind his antagonism toward his mother.

"Come in and meet Mr. Mercer," Alanna invited Mike and me.

We had to come into the room and be introduced. Harry Mercer didn't seem interested in us, so I told Alanna that we had to be going and reminded her about the autograph. The afternoon had gone all too fast. I'd had no time with Alanna alone, no time to get acquainted with her, no opportunity to talk about me. And now that Mr. Mercer was there to take her attention, I knew that couldn't be changed. It was all very disappointing.

She had brought a sheet of her personal notepaper into the room, and a pen to sign it with. She sat down at a desk and wrote a few lines on the paper, saying that she'd enjoyed meeting me and that she hoped to see more of me. Then she looked up and smiled.

"You'll come back and visit Steven again, won't you?" she said. "You and your brother?"

I wanted to jump at that and ask her when we could come again, but I didn't quite dare. Our visit hadn't been successful so far as I was concerned, but I smiled back at her brightly and nodded. Maybe I could have another chance.

"Good," she said. "We haven't had much opportunity to get acquainted, have we? I haven't even answered any questions you might have liked to ask."

Clearly she knew about fans, knew they were full of questions. I spoke quickly, snatching at an opportunity.

"I've wondered how you got to be an actress. How did you begin? What was your first chance, and all that?"

She seemed to stiffen just a little. Her eyes no longer looked as though she had been crying, but they still looked sad, and they didn't warm to my questions.

"Perhaps we can talk another time," she said. "It's all a long story. And perhaps a bit boring anyway. I really don't know why anyone would be interested."

I plunged in. I didn't take the time to think or question my own words. I just blurted them out.

"I'm interested because I want to be an actress," I said.

At that moment a silence fell in the room, and I knew with my own shocked ears that everyone had heard me. Harry Mercer was unimpressed. Mike looked ashamed of me. And Steven was smiling as though this was something he would enjoy making fun of. But

Alanna was kind. She didn't even say that a good many young girls got stagestruck at some time or another—which was what my mother had said. She just looked sympathetic and kind.

"We'll have to talk about that," she told me. "Now you'll surely have to come back." But still she didn't mention a time.

We said good-by and went into the hall. Daphne Price stood near the drawing room door and I knew that she too had heard my remark. Under her red hair her face looked dark and disapproving. I knew that for some reason she did not like me and didn't want me to come back again. She went with us to the door silently and let us out, only nodding when we told her a polite good-by.

The sun was down by the time we went outside, and the woods were shadowy with the promise of coming night. I walked so fast that Mike had to hurry to keep up with me.

"Well, what did you think of them all?" I asked him as we walked along.

But Mike, who could dig beneath the surface of any kind of machinery, did not always dig below the surface with people. "Oh, I guess they're all right," he said. "Though except for Alanna Graham nobody was very friendly."

That, at least, was true, I thought as we left the woods and walked up the hill toward home. When we reached the front steps Mike went inside, but I walked around in back. I didn't want to go in right away and be questioned by Gram about our visit. There was too much I didn't want to say to Gram.

Joe Reed was outside working on storm windows and he looked up from his work when I appeared. He didn't say anything but just waited as though he expected me to begin to talk. Because he was outside the family and wouldn't be likely to criticize me, I did start to talk.

I was boiling over with words, and it didn't matter if he thought I was a little crazy.

"Do you believe in spooky things?" I asked him.

His fingers were busy and he didn't look at me. "I don't suppose I do, if you mean ghosts and that sort of thing. Have you been meeting any?"

"Not exactly. There's an old man living down in that house below us—" I pointed. "Burton Oliver. He used to do a lot of sculpturing. I don't know if he was famous or anything, but they've got a whole room down there filled with figures he carved long ago. They're packed into his old studio, and he makes everybody who goes in there lock the door and hang the key on a hook outside. So nothing will get out of the room. That's what he said."

Joe's thin face was expressionless. "Old men get funny ideas."

"But the figures he made are strange. Weird. Some of them are fighting demons and dragons. Some of them look terrified, as though they were being tormented in some way."

"I remember," Joe said unexpectedly. "I saw a Burton Oliver sculpture in a museum once. It was of an eagle attacking a man. And you're right—it was pretty weird."

Joe didn't look like the sort of person who would go into a museum, so that was surprising. He looked like another stray—like most of Gramp's handymen.

"But figures like that can't really have a life of their own the way he thinks," I said.

Joe answered shortly. "I don't suppose so." Then he picked up a storm sash and carried it away, leaving me standing there. It hadn't been a satisfactory talk, but I couldn't have expected anything more. I didn't even know Joe very well.

I went thoughtfully inside the house. How soon could I see Alanna again, and would she ever really talk to me? I took off my outdoor things and left them on the rack near the door.

"Oh, there you are," Gram called to me. She was sitting on the couch in the living room, working on some needlepoint. "How was your party?"

"All right, I guess. Steven showed us around the house a little. But we didn't play any games or anything. We just sat and talked."

Gram set her needlepoint aside. "It's probably a good idea for children to sit down now and then and learn how to carry on a conversation. You talk enough at mealtime around here. Jan, how would you and Mike like to go into Stroudsburg tomorrow morning and do some Christmas shopping?"

I might have jumped at the chance, but another idea had begun to tempt me. Alanna had said she and Steven were going skiing tomorrow.

"I'd like to get Gramp to take us skiing in the morning," I said. "Maybe we'd better catch this good weather while it lasts. Could we shop in the afternoon?"

Gram nodded. "It should do just as well. Anyway, it will depend on how I'm feeling. And now, how would you like to help me start dinner?"

I always liked to work with Gram in the kitchen. It was a little like working under a general, because her plans were always laid out so well, and she usually moved about briskly, overseeing everything and at the same time chopping, stirring, and mixing things efficiently herself. While she was busy directing me, I could think.

About Alanna's tears, for one thing, and about that peculiar mention of a phone call. About the way she hadn't wanted to talk to Steven about it but had blurted out something to Mr. Mercer right away. And about the edgy, uncomfortable feeling between Steven and his mother. I had a curious sense that Steven loved and hated her at the same time, and that her son's behavior left Alanna sad and baffled. I was glad there was no feeling like that between Mike and me and our parents. I also thought about the way I had less than two weeks before I would have to go home to being nobody again. That was the worst thing of all.

Maybe you don't know what that's really like in a family like mine. Everyone outside keeps saying, "Oh, how wonderful to be Kay Sutton's daughter! And to have Clifford Sutton for a father! Wasn't it your brother, Michael, whom we saw on television a few weeks ago? How exciting to live in a family like that! And what do *you* do?"

This isn't a little, unimportant thing that will be automatically taken care of when I grow up. I want to *be somebody now*. Or at least to show some sort of promise in some direction. And Alanna might be able to help me. She knew all about becoming an actress. I wondered if she had wanted to be one when she was very young, and if her father and mother had opposed her.

That reminded me of another thing. The terrible way Alanna's grandmother had fallen to her death from the window of her husband's studio. When had that happened? I wondered. Had Alanna been grown up by then? Had she been at home? Steven had been hushed when he started to talk about it, but he'd mentioned it again later when we were in the studio. I shivered, and Gram asked if I was cold. I wasn't, of course. It was just that my thoughts had taken a chilly turn ever since we'd visited the Oliver house.

At dinner that night I asked Gramp about skiing in the morning, and he said we could go over to the ski area right after breakfast if we wanted to. So that was set. If I could see Alanna on the slopes, perhaps she would set a definite time when we could come and visit Steven again. Only this time I would find a way to have a talk with her at the house.

I wondered how I could prove myself worth her interest. At home sometimes I read speeches out of plays aloud to myself while I stood in front of a mirror. I thought I was pretty good. Really dramatic, sometimes. I wondered if I could read any lines for Alanna. That set me off into a long daydream while I ate a dinner I hardly tasted, and I imagined Alanna being astonished by my talent and assuring me that I should have every encouragement. It was a good thing that Gramp talked most of his way through dinner, so that nobody noticed that I wasn't really there.

The evening seemed long because I was anxious to be out on the slopes again, watching for Steven and his mother. But it finally passed and I got ready for bed. After I turned out my lights I stepped out on the balcony with a coat over my pajamas and looked down at that spooky old house. I wondered what it would be like to have to spend a night there, and I didn't dream that before long I'd be doing that very thing. A few lights burned, both upstairs and downstairs, but there was none in Steven's room.

When I came back to bed I was too drowsy to think about anything much, and I quickly sank into a deep sleep. What awakened me in the middle of the night was a terrible, fierce barking. It came from the direction of the Oliver house. I rolled right out of bed and grabbed my coat before I rushed out into the cold. The stars were bright overheard and there was a lopsided moon. All sorts of lights were coming on down in the house, and someone was shouting. That was Thor barking, and he was raising the very roof.

Through the many windows that had no closed draperies or blinds, I could see people running about the rooms. A light came on in Steven's room, but there the blinds were closed so I couldn't see anything. A man's voice shouted at Thor—that was probably Mr. Mercer—and after a while everything quieted down. In our house I could hear Gramp moving around, so I knew he must be up and looking out of a window too.

It was so cold my breath made a white cloud on the glittery air. I couldn't stay out there, and the disturbance, whatever it was, must be over. But just before I stepped back into my room, I saw a shadow move down in our yard. Someone had come up the driveway. As I watched he let himself into the garage apartment and disappeared. Joe Reed, of course.

Had he come out because of all the barking or had he been out all the time? Had he, I wondered, shivering, been down near the Oliver house? And if he had, what for?

I was beginning to think of Joe Reed as a rather sinister character. There was the way he kept to himself and acted a little strange, not always friendly. I tried to remember what he had said to me about Burton Oliver and his sculpture. He had agreed that it was weird and he had mentioned seeing a piece that represented an eagle attacking a man. That would be just like the others I'd seen.

When I was back in bed, I couldn't put the memory of that room filled with figures out of my mind. I could imagine their monstrous shadows all too clearly, moving around down there in the moon-filled darkness. Maybe it was a good thing that a key was kept outside the door, so that all those horrors were kept locked safely in one room. Let them do their moonlit dance under the skylight behind a locked door.

I wondered about my reluctance to tell Gramp and Gram about all the things that had happened that day, and how we had been received at the Oliver house. Perhaps I felt that they wouldn't want Mike and me to go down there again when everything was so strange and out of the ordinary. But perhaps the time had come to talk to Gramp. Especially about Joe Reed. I felt a little more comfortable when I'd decided that, and I finally went back to sleep.

—6

A Visitor

In the morning there was no time to catch Gramp before we had breakfast and set out for the slopes. I wanted to talk to him alone, without Mike there to put in his own ideas and probably laugh at mine and criticize me.

Apparently we reached the slopes earlier than Alanna did, because nobody from the big house was in sight on the runs. I tramped around through crusty snow at the foot of each run, watching the early skiers coming down the mountain and going up again. And I didn't see anyone I knew. I had separated from Mike and Gramp to go my own way. I had my chair-lift ticket fastened to the outside of my parka, so I could go up and down as I pleased, and Gramp made no effort to hold us together. He understood that some of the fun of skiing is the wonderful sense you get of being alone and on your own. We could meet easily at the bottom of the chair, so there was no difficulty about not finding each other. And in case of serious accidents, men from the ski patrol were always on duty.

I was just about to line up for the chair lift when I saw the first of Alanna's party come around one end of the base lodge. It was Harry Mercer, and for me he wasn't a welcome sight. He saw me too, but pretended he didn't, and I didn't like him any the better for that. After him came Daphne Price, and that was a surprise. Instead of wearing her usual black, she wore an orange parka and brown pants, and she seemed much more lively and interested in what she was doing than she had back at the house.

Next came Steven in green, with Alanna winding up the rear. Today she wore an all-red outfit and you could see her a mile away. She was even more brilliant than Cousin Daphne. Mr. Mercer wore dark blue and looked very handsome and hawklike, and as though he was not unused to skiing.

Quickly I got myself out of the way where Alanna's party wouldn't notice me, because, if possible, I wanted to see Steven alone. If I could catch him by himself in a good moment, perhaps he'd set a date when I could come to see him again. Eventually I got into line behind Alanna, but she didn't notice me. She looked around all the time, as if she was watching for something or someone, but she simply saw me as a young girl. She didn't recognize me with my hood over my eyes.

Mr. Mercer and Cousin Daphne got into the first chair, and Alanna and Steven got into the next one. There was no crowd yet, so I managed to get a chair alone, swinging right along after Alanna and Steven in their green and red. I was safe enough going up, because it was hard to turn around and look back along the lift line. I wanted to see if I could catch Steven alone somewhere at the top.

But they seemed not to leave him alone for a moment. They all schussed down the ramp and out along the top of the runs. I snowplowed after them, hanging back a little. Mike was up there, I saw. He had discovered a snow maker that looked like a machine gun on a tripod. It wasn't working that day, and he was down on his hands and knees examining it, while the blue hose snaked away down the mountain.

Alanna saw him and called out. Then Alanna's

party stopped to talk to Mike for a minute. At least Alanna and Steven did. I had an idea that Mr. Mercer was bored, and Cousin Daphne was not pleased. When they went on toward Hemlock, which is the run next to Devil's Drop and where the slope isn't so steep, I pushed along after them. There they stood around arguing among themselves, as though they couldn't decide who was to go down first.

Finally Cousin Daphne went ahead and I saw that she was a really good skier. Alanna followed, and Steven and Mr. Mercer were left. I supposed Steven would be sent down next, with Harry winding up the rear guard, so I decided to make my presence known, rather than miss altogether a chance to speak to Steven.

"Hi, Steven!" I called, and snowplowed out where he could see me.

He looked around and waved a ski pole at me. I'm sure he would have come toward me, but Mr. Mercer grabbed him by the arm.

"Your mother wanted you to go right down," he said, "so we can all stay together. Get started, and I'll follow you."

Steven looked mad, and I knew he would hate to be pushed around by this man. He rolled his eyes at me as though he was trying to tell me something and then poled himself down the slope. I watched as Mr. Mercer started after him. Suddenly Steven edged his skis, whisked himself off to the side of the slope, and bent as if to adjust a binding. Mr. Mercer didn't have time to stop. He went past Steven in a flash. I saw my chance, skated to the top of the run to give myself a start, and pushed myself down. But I didn't go fast. When I came to where Steven had stopped, I too got off the main slope and out of the way of anyone who might be coming behind me. Below, Mr. Mercer slid into a spray of snow, and I knew he'd be climbing back to us in a moment.

"I wanted to see you," I called to Steven. "Maybe you can help me. I want to talk to your mother about something. When can we come back to see you again?"

Steven was unpredictable. I had no idea whether he'd scowl at my suggestion or welcome it. But perhaps he was a little bored down in that big house. He cast a glance toward Mr. Mercer, sidestepping up the slope with his skis across the fall line. It wasn't a very fast way to move, but there was no way to come up a slope quickly on skis.

"What do you want to see my mother about?" he asked. "Being an actress?"

So he'd remembered that. And he was grinning for once instead of scowling. Though it wasn't exactly a pleasant grin.

"It's awfully important to me," I said in a little rush. "You don't know what it's like in my family, with everyone famous but me, and—"

"Oh, don't I?" he said. For the first time he looked almost sympathetic, because he had a famous mother too. "Why don't you come again tomorrow afternoon? We're going to be out today."

"Will your mother care?"

"*I'm* inviting you," Steven said.

That seemed to settle the matter—and just in time, because Mr. Mercer had reached us. He bent over Steven's binding to see if anything was wrong and frowned at me.

"What are you doing here?" he demanded, as though Steven's stopping was my fault.

I felt like telling him the slopes were free, but Steven had started down, so I didn't answer. I went straight after him. Mr. Mercer was left to follow us as he pleased.

It was astonishing to watch Steven ski. He might

have trouble walking, he might limp ordinarily, but on skis he was terrific. His built-up boot held his bad foot securely, and he seemed to have expert control. He carved around the moguls like a pro, and his christys and edging were very good. I was busy getting myself down, so I couldn't pay too close attention, but I saw enough to know that he was fine on skis, just as his mother had said. When I schussed after him at the bottom, Mr. Mercer came after us to where the others were waiting. Steven went right over to his mother.

"Is it all right if Mike and Jan come over tomorrow afternoon?" he asked.

Alanna looked pleased and spoke to me brightly. "That will be fine. We'll be glad to see you."

Cousin Daphne sulked a little, and Mr. Mercer let his expression go blank, so I knew we weren't entirely welcome. But Alanna had said we could come, so that was enough.

I saw Gramp a little way off and waved to him. He poled himself over and spoke to Alanna, introducing himself, and she introduced him to the others, seeming warmly pleased to meet him, even if they weren't. I wondered what was the matter with that household, and why there were all those gloomy dispositions around. I wondered how Alanna could stand those two. Oddly enough, Cousin Daphne and Harry Mercer didn't even seem to like each other very much, though sometimes I caught them whispering together.

When Gramp had talked to her for a while, Alanna led her party over to the lift for another turn down the mountain, and I was left with Gramp. Mike was probably still up at the top checking over that snow maker, so here was my chance.

"I need to talk to you, Gramp," I said. "I need to talk to you alone."

He didn't ask any questions but just nodded at me solemnly, and we headed for the lodge. We knew

Mike was perfectly happy on his own, so Gramp and I went inside and sat down at a wooden table with bowls of steaming-hot clam chowder before us. While we crumbled crackers and ate our soup, I tried to tell Gramp all that was worrying me. Except for one thing. I didn't want to tell him how much I wanted to be an actress. I had a feeling that no grown-up except Alanna was going to understand and take me seriously.

I told him about the spooky atmosphere of the house and about the locked room that contained Burton Oliver's sculptures. I told him about Cousin Daphen's unfriendliness, and about the way Mr. Mercer either paid no attention to us or seemed impatient about having us around. Yet all the while Alanna was really welcoming.

"That's what counts," Gramp said. "I should think she'd like to have you keep Steven company. If those two grownups aren't pleased, it doesn't matter too much, just so long as you try not to provoke them. I don't know that there's any big mystery about their behavior. Some people just don't care for children."

As for my feeling of spookiness, he smiled over that. "Isn't it sometimes fun to scare ourselves? I can remember doing it when I was a boy. When you get used to the house, you probably won't give all this a second thought."

Though I had a feeling that I would, I didn't try to argue with him but went on to tell him the next thing— the thing I was uneasy about mentioning. About Joe Reed's interest in the house down the hill, and how I'd seen him creeping around in the dark last night after all the uproar in the big house.

Gramp took this mildly enough. "You sometimes let your imagination go, Jan. I don't think we need to worry about Joe. He talked to me a little about himself before I took him on, and I know he's going through a time of wanting to be alone. I think he doesn't sleep well at night, so it's natural for him to get up and wander about."

"You don't think he went down to the Oliver place and started all that uproar with Thor?"

"I shouldn't think so," Gramp said. "But why don't you ask him?"

I didn't care for that idea, and I felt that Gramp was altogether too easygoing. I knew he made a point of trusting people. But before I could object, Gramp nodded toward the window beside us, with its great view of the slopes.

"There's Mike. You'd better go let him know where we are."

I pulled on my parka and in my ski boots went clumping out of the room and down the outside stairs. I called to Mike and he came to join us, getting a bowl of clam chowder from the counter. After that we didn't talk any more about the problems of the house down the hill, though I kept on feeling terribly uneasy inside.

Talking to Gramp hadn't solved anything. There was still some sort of mystery, a serious, dark, frightening mystery, hanging over that house. Alanna was disturbed about something, and I didn't think Mr. Mercer or Cousin Daphne were to be trusted. I didn't know what they were after.

Anyway, I was going back there for another visit tomorrow, and though the fact sent a little shiver down my spine, I was glad to be going. Maybe there was even something I could do for Steven, shut up in that huge, dark old house, and not very happy there.

When we had finished our soup, we went back for more skiing. I didn't see Steven again close up. Alanna had her group skiing on Hemlock. All the runs in ski areas are named so that skiers can talk about the different slopes. There was a big map at the foot of these slopes that showed all the runs, so you could get to know the territory.

After a while we went home for lunch, and then Gram drove Mike and me to Stroudsburg to do some Christmas shopping in the bigger shops in that town. It wasn't like shopping in New York, but we had our Christmas money with us and we bought a few things we thought Gram and Gramp would like. Our main Christmas preparations for Mother and Dad had been made back in New York.

That evening something peculiar happened. Something that made me worry about Joe all over again, no matter what Gramp had said. And it made me worry about Harry Mercer too.

After dinner Mike got out his guitar and said he was going over to play some tunes with Joe. It developed that Joe had a guitar too, and that he played and sang, and he had invited Mike over.

"He said you could come too, if you want to," Mike told me.

So we let Gramp know where we were going, and when we left the house he came along to listen and enjoy the music. Just because our parents think classical music is the only kind in the world doesn't mean that Mike and I don't appreciate other kinds too. We listen to a lot of pop music on the air and on records, especially when Mother isn't home to make faces. We keep trying to get her to listen to the words so that she'll understand better. We like folk rock and country music, and Joe played some on his guitar that night, with Mike joining in.

Joe sat on a stool in his next-to-the-garage room, with a shock of sandy hair falling down his forehead as he bent over his guitar in that way players have, as though they love their instruments. His thin face still looked closed and dark, but his eyes didn't seem as desperate as they sometimes did. Mike sat on a lower stool, with his legs sprawled out in their jeans, while Gramp took the only chair, working on a piece of carving in spite of his crippled hands, exercising them. There was a round, central table with small green pottery lamp on it that Gram had brought out for Joe to use, and Gramp's gray head looked very handsome in the soft light. Since it didn't matter what I sat on, I chose the woodpile and pulled up my knees so my chin could rest on them while I watched and listened.

Joe had the potbellied stove going, its sides glowing with warmth, so that his small place was snug, even though the wind had begun to howl outdoors. It was a cozy night for singing, and Joe had a good voice. A quiet voice that could do well with the ballad type of song. He crooned "Where Have All the Flowers Gone?" so sadly that it made me want to cry. And he sang John Lennon's "Yesterday," and one of Rod McKuen's songs. Finally he launched into something mournful about a lost child who couldn't find his mother, and it seemed that he had made that one up himself.

Mike was good at picking up a tune by ear, and he began to accompany Joe on his long, sad song. Wood burned and crackled in the hot little stove, and outside the wind moaned and slapped branches against the garage. It was all lovely and peaceful until that knock came on the door.

Joe looked up from his guitar in a startled way and made no move to go to the door. Whoever was there rapped again, and Mike jumped up and went to answer the knock. He opened the door a crack on that howling wind, and I could see Harry Mercer's pale face over my brother's head.

"Is your grandfather here?" Mr. Mercer asked.

Mike stepped back to let him in, and Gramp rose to greet him. That was when I noticed that Joe had vanished. One minute he was there with his guitar, but while I looked toward Mr. Mercer through the crack of open door, he had gone, his guitar left leaning against against the stool. I knew there was a door back there that led into the garage and other doors from the garage that led outside. His jacket was gone from its peg too, so he must have taken himself off in one smooth movement before Harry Mercer had been brought into the room.

Mr. Mercer looked cold, and he didn't wait for anybody to invite him over to the stove. He just came in, and after a brief greeting to Gramp, began to warm his hands. He paid no attention to Mike and me.

"Mrs. Clausen said you were over here," he told Gramp. "Miss Graham asked me to give you a message."

"Yes, of course," Gramp said. "I hope nothing is wrong."

Mr. Mercer talked over his shoulder while he stood at the stove, not looking at us. He didn't seem to know about Joe, or that he was missing.

"Steven isn't very strong," he said. "And this morning on the slopes was too much for him. It isn't advisable for him to have company tomorrow, and Miss Graham asked me to come and let you know."

Steven had looked anything but tired on the runs today, and I wondered why his mother hadn't phoned herself to change our plans. None of the electric wires were down in spite of the wind, and probably the phone wasn't out either. His coming over in the cold to tell us this seemed a little strange. I felt terribly disappointed, and questioning too. I didn't know whether I believed Harry Mercer.

"I'm sorry about that," Gramp said, looking at me. "But I'm sure Jan and Mike will understand. Maybe another time."

"Perhaps," Mr. Mercer said, sounding as though he meant never.

He seemed reluctant to go back into the wind and the cold, but there didn't seem to be anything else to do, so he backed away from the stove and started for the door.

Gramp got up to open the door but paused with his hand on the knob. "Quite a disturbance down at your place last night," he said. "Was anything wrong?"

Mr. Mercer grunted unpleasantly. His strong nose looked more like a hawk's beak than ever, and his gray eyes were sharp. "Prowlers, we think. The dog was upset about something. If I'd caught sight of anyone, I'd have taken a shot at him."

That sounded pretty bloodthirsty. And the prowler thing was unusual out here in the country. I wondered what had really happened.

Anyway, Mr. Mercer took himself off with a quick, "Good night," and when the door closed after him, we all looked at each other uneasily. Mike picked up his guitar and strummed a few chords, quickly lost in his own interest. I spoke my thoughts aloud.

"I wonder if Alanna really sent him to tell us not to come," I said.

Gramp seemed to consider this. "At least it's pretty definite that somebody doesn't want you down there tomorrow."

But he didn't tell me not to go, and I had a feeling that I wanted to find out about that message for myself. For some reason Harry Mercer seemed to have taken a special dislike to me, and I didn't understand why.

In a minute or two Joe came back inside, looking cold from standing in the unheated garage. He took off his jacket without saying anything, picked up his guitar again, and sat on the stool. None of us asked any questions, and he didn't explain his sudden departure at Mr. Mercer's appearance. I just didn't feel comfortable about him, and when he began to play and sing again, with Mike joining in, I found myself staring at him curiously, wondering about him even more. It seemed strange that he hadn't wanted to meet Mr. Mercer. And that he'd been up and around when the dogs were barking last night. I hope he wouldn't give someone down at the house a chance to take a shot at him.

Gramp seemed undisturbed and he was busy with his carving again, working over a piece of newspaper on his knees, so he could dump shavings in the fire now and then. Joe's songs turned to country and folk rock, but I found I wasn't enjoying the coziness of the evening anymore, so I stood up.

"I'm getting sleepy. I think I'll go to bed."

Gramp nodded at me pleasantly, and I went to kiss him good night. The others stayed on as I walked out into the howling wind. There was the cold of winter in the blast. I pulled my jacket tight at the throat and scooted across the yard to the side door.

Gram was in the living room, reading a book. "I could hear the music, dear," she said. "It sounded lovely. I'm glad that Joe Reed is fitting in so well. Some of the men Gramp finds to work here aren't very friendly."

I wasn't sure that Joe was truly friendly. I only knew there was something strange about him.

"Is there anything wrong with the phone?" I said, going into the hall to pick up the receiver. The dial tone came on at once. There was nothing wrong.

"Would you like some warm milk and crackers before you go to bed?" Gram asked.

That sounded fine, so I went into the kitchen with her while she warmed the milk, and before I had finished drinking it, Gramp and Mike came in from the garage. Neither one seemed upset about anything, and I went up to bed wondering if what I felt was all imaginary—just something inside my head.

—7

Fresh Attack

There was no barking dog that night—only the wind rising in a gale and bringing a scattering of snow with it before morning. When I woke up I lay for a while thinking about what I meant to do that afternoon. My suspicion of Harry Mercer hadn't changed and I didn't feel that I wanted to accept his canceling of Steven's invitation without even checking.

The day seemed a long one to get through. I wrapped my Christmas packages and did what chores I could to help Gram, who wasn't feeling well again. But when teatime came, the hour when we were supposed to have gone down to the Oliver house, I told everyone I was going for a walk, and I set out down the hill.

Once more there was no one on the driveway through the woods, and I hurried through the dark trees as fast as I could go. When I banged the door knocker, Cousin Daphne came to open the door, and we stared at each other with mutual distrust.

"You weren't supposed to come," she said.

"I know," I told her. "I just came to see Miss Graham."

She looked gloomy again this afternoon out of her orange parka and back in her black dress, with only her red hair glowing in the light from overhead. For the first time I noticed how dark her eyes were, as if they caught no light, so that they too were black with gloom. What made her like that? I wondered. Would I feel more kindly toward her if I understood her feelings and thoughts? I didn't know.

Perhaps my staring made her uncomfortable, because after a moment she stepped back from the doorway, however reluctantly.

"All right," she said. "Come in and wait here. I'll go and see."

I stepped into the big square hall and watched her black figure as it climbed the stairs. But I didn't watch for long, because no sooner had she gone than Thor came bounding in through an open door from another part of the house. He began to bark as soon as he saw me, and he advanced on me with his eyes glaring and his lips drawn back from his teeth in a snarl.

There was no one to call for help, and I wasn't going to stand there and face him. Against a nearby wall stood a chest of drawers that came almost to my shoulder. A drawer at the bottom was partly open, making a step. I flew toward it and clambered up its face to scramble onto the top. Thor came leaping after me, but I was just out of his reach. In my haste I knocked against the big Greek jar on top of the chest and it tipped and rocked ominously. I tried to catch it in time to save it from falling, but it slipped out of my hands and went off into the air, crashing to the floor. The echoes of that crash seemed to go on forever as the jar fell apart.

I stood on top of the chest, looking down in horror. Even Thor must have been startled into silence, because he stopped barking and he too stared at the broken pieces of the jar.

Steven's voice spoke to me from the stairs. "You're in trouble now. That's my mother's favorite jar and it's very valuable."

"If your dog hadn't come after me, I wouldn't have knocked it over," I said crossly.

"Thor won't hurt you. He just makes a lot of noise. Anyway, you look silly up there. You'd better come down."

Feeling thoroughly ruffled and not trusting Thor at all, I sat down on the chest and swung my legs. "The pieces are big ones. Perhaps they can be glued together."

"That's not the same thing," Steven said. He came down the stairs, limping a little, and collared Thor to drag him across the hall. When he had thrust the dog through a door, he closed it after him. "You can come down now."

I jumped to the floor and knelt beside the broken pieces of the Greek jar. I felt awful about breaking it but annoyed with Steven at the same time. Then something among the pieces caught my eye and I reached out to pick it up. It was a flat envelope of the sort that photographers use to mail small pictures.

"Look," I said. "There's something in the jar."

Steven took the envelope from my hand and opened it. It contained a gray folder about five by seven that framed a picture. I was interested now because it seemed strange that anyone would have dropped the envelope into that jar, so I stood close beside Steven, looking over his shoulder as he opened the folder. The picture inside was only a news photo, cut out of some paper, though it was framed by the folder. It showed a young woman coming down the steps of an official-looking building, with an older woman walking beside her. The young woman looked frightened, the older one grim. Even though she was years younger, there was no mistaking the identity of the first woman. It was Alanna Graham when she must have been about eighteen.

"It's your mother!" I said. "Why would anybody—"

But Steven broke in on me tensely. "It's none of your business. I'll take care of this."

He closed the folder and slipped it back in its brown envelope. Then he stared at me almost defiantly.

"Why didn't you want to come over today? Mr. Mercer said you sent word you couldn't come."

I could only gape at him. "But I thought you were too tired to have company. When Mr. Mercer came up to our place last night he said your mother didn't want you to have company today."

Steven stared back at me as realization dawned on us. For some reason Harry Mercer hadn't wanted me to come, and he had tried to arrange it so I wouldn't be able to.

"I didn't believe him last night," I said. "That's why I came anyway today—to find out. What do you suppose he's up to? Why should he want to keep Mike and me away?"

Before Steven could answer, Cousin Daphne came down the stairs and took in everything at once—smashed jar and all. She ran toward the broken pieces a little frantically.

"How awful! What happened? Alanna will be devastated!"

Her look rested on the envelope in Steven's hands. "What's that?" she asked.

"Something of mine," Steven said, and echoed what I had offered earlier. "The jar broke into big pieces. Let's pick them up and see if they can be glued together." He tucked the envelope under one arm and knelt to gather the jagged bits together.

"Never mind," Cousin Daphne said. "I'll take care of it. But you'd better go tell your mother. I don't want to." Then she spoke to me. "Miss Graham isn't feeling well, and she can't see you today."

"But Steven can see me," I said a little defiantly.

Cousin Daphne looked furious. Apparently she didn't want me in the house any more than Harry Mercer did, but she was blocked by Steven and couldn't do much about it.

"Come along," Steven said, and led the way upstairs.

I followed him eagerly, glad to get away from both Cousin Daphne and the calamity of that broken jar. Though I knew I still had to cope with that.

"When should I tell your mother?" I asked Steven as we reached the head of the stairs.

"Wait a minute," he said and darted off toward his room. When he came back his hands were empty, and I knew he had put that strange folder away. "You might as well talk to her now and tell her what you did," he said as he rejoined me.

"But if she's not feeling well—"

"You'd better tell her anyway," he said, sounding as grim as Cousin Daphne.

There was nothing to do but follow him toward his mother's room. It was on the second floor, and when he knocked on the door, she called to him to come in, her voice faint.

The room we entered was a sitting room, with an adjoining bedroom that I could see through an open door. Alanna Graham lay back in a chaise longue upholstered in rose, her feet on a pillow and her eyes covered with a damp cloth. She wore a primrose yellow robe that glowed like a spot of sunlight. Beside her a fire burned in the small grate below a pink marble mantelpiece. Harry Mercer was across the room, sitting in an easy chair reading a newspaper. He gave me a sour look as I stepped through the door behind Steven.

"Your mother isn't feeling well," he began.

"I know," Steven said, making it sound as though he didn't care. "But Jan has to tell her something."

Alanna took the cloth from her eyes and blinked at the light. "I'm all right," she said. "Hello, Jan. What is it, dear?"

Everything was wrong as usual. If Alanna had a headache, this wasn't the right time to talk to her about what I really wanted to discuss. And besides, both Mr. Mercer and Steven were there. In any case, I had something more urgent that had to be talked about.

"I—I had an accident downstairs," I said.

"An accident? I'm sorry."

"It was Thor's fault." Steven came unexpectedly to my aid. "He barked and jumped around and scared her so that—"

But I had to tell this myself. "So I climbed up on a chest to get away from the dog, and I—I knocked over that Greek jar and broke it. Steven says it's valuable—and—"

Alanna waved one hand weakly, dismissing the matter. "Don't concern yourself, Jan. That jar was given to me by someone I didn't like very well. So don't worry about it."

"I think the pieces can be glued together—it didn't break into small bits," I said. I felt relieved, yet at the same time not altogether reassured. I had the feeling that at another time Alanna might have felt much worse about the jar. Right now something else was worrying her so badly that she had no feeling left over for a Greek jar.

Harry Mercer was watching us over his newspaper, but he didn't speak to me or say anything. Steven started for the door and there was nothing to do but follow him. He crossed the hall and went into a room that was clearly his own. It, too, was a sitting room, with a bedroom opening off it. But Steven's was an activity room, with a table in the center that had a checkerborard set into it like a mosaic and chairs pulled up around it. There were shelves of books and games, and a small desk with writing things and a note-book laid out on it.

Steven ignored everything and ignored me as well. He went across to a window and stared up the hill toward where Gramp's house rose on the mountainside, visible through openings in the trees.

"We heard all the rumpus down here the other night," I said. "What was Thor barking about?"

"Who knows?" Steven was gruff. "It could have been anything. Mr. Mercer has prowlers on the brain. I didn't see anyone, and I got up right away to look."

That seemed to end that subject.

"I'm afraid I've upset your mother," I said unhappily. "I was hoping to talk to her today, but now she isn't going to think much of me."

He looked around at me. "Oh, yes—about your acting ambition—is that it?"

I didn't want to talk to him about that and I was silent.

"Anyway, she was already upset," he said, and took a quick, restless turn about the room.

To get out of his way I sat down in one of the chairs at the checker table. He seemed to be talking to himself more than to me, so I listened quietly.

"I don't know what's got into her," he went on. "She's had some queer phone calls and afterward she cries and won't talk to anyone."

I couldn't help making a comment. "Maybe you upset her. You don't seem to treat her very niccly."

His old scowl came back and he turned it on me ferociously. "She's a fake!" he said angrily. "She thinks she's so perfect that she can condemn my father and keep him away from me. She's no good and—"

"I think she's wonderful," I countered indignantly. "I think you're awfully lucky to have her for your mother."

His scowl deepened. "What do you know about it?"

He swung himself around the room again and came to a halt close to the table. "You think she's like all those silly movies. All that stuff about being good and noble and generous and kind! Real people aren't like that."

"I don't suppose they are," I said.

"Well, don't you care? Don't you mind when someone pretends to be good and isn't?"

"Are you good all the time?" I asked him.

"That's different. I don't pretend to be."

"I think you're the one who is making her unhappy. I think she worries about you."

"That's fine! I'd like her to worry. It would serve her right."

What a strange, unhappy boy he was. I couldn't help trying to put myself in his mixed-up state. I was worried about how he felt and I wished I could help him to stop feeling that way. But trying didn't really help me to understand Steven. There seemed something strange and terribly wrong about his behavior.

"I think your mother loves you a great deal," I said as gently as I could.

He made a growling sound deep in his throat, a little like Thor. "How can she love me, or be proud of me, or anything, when—" he broke off and turned his back on me, stalked to the window, limping and stumbling over nothing, as though he had run into something on the floor.

This was a different road he had turned down. First he was set against his mother because, he said, she wasn't like the role she played in pictures. Now he was saying that she couldn't be proud of him, perhaps couldn't love him, because he had a bad leg and wasn't like other boys. Perhaps he believed in both ends of this scale and they added up to a weight he couldn't carry. I wanted very much to help him but I didn't know how.

"Maybe you don't give her much chance to be

proud of you," I said. "Anyway, I know how you feel. Because that's the way it is in my family too. Everybody else can do something. My dad and mother are proud of each other, and they're proud of Mike because he can sing and play the guitar, and he understands about engines and things too. But I can't do anything."

Ordinarily these weren't things I'd have told anyone. But I thought telling them might help Steven. He might see that others could be in the same mess too.

But he only snorted as though nothing I said mattered in comparison to his own troubles. He was a very self-centered boy.

I'd just about come to the conclusion that I'd better go home and start writing a letter to Dad about the breaking of the Greek jar. I couldn't simply let it go. Something would have to be done to recompense Alanna for its loss. But at that moment she came in from the hall, the soft yellow color of her robe flowing around her beautifully as she moved. Her black hair was caught at the back of her neck with a yellow ribbon and hung long down her back.

"Oh, you're still here, Jan," she said. "I was afraid I'd be too late to catch you. My head's better now, so we can have our little talk. Will you come back with me to my sitting room?"

My heart gave a huge thump in my chest. I couldn't have been more pleased, though Steven looked thoroughly disgruntled. I had a feeling that he didn't want me to be friends with his mother, and I wished I could win him over. She held out her hand to me and took my arm.

"You'll excuse us, Steven? Jan and I have something to talk about."

He said nothing as we returned to the sitting room. Mr. Mercer was gone and Alanna lay back on the rose-colored chaise longue, her gown shimmering yellow against its glow, and gestured me to a chair at her side.

The wood fire in the small grate crackled cheerfully, bathing the room in soft rosy light. Alanna seemed to be trying very hard to be her normal self.

"So you want to be an actress?" she said.

The way she spoke the words didn't sound silly, and I knew she wasn't laughing at me.

"I think I could be one," I told her softly.

"Why? Why do you think that?"

I thought about her question for a moment. "Perhaps because I like to imagine being other people. I think I could pretend to be other people."

"A very interesting reason," she said. "But most actors don't start out as young as you are."

"Didn't you?"

She shook her head. "I was in my early twenties when I first thought about singing and dancing. Even then I didn't think about acting at first. That came after I went out to Hollywood. I won a small beauty contest and they sent me out to the West Coast to take a screen test. I wasn't very good, but the studio gave me a small part in a picture."

"Oh," I said, disappointed, "a beauty contest . . ."

"That's sometimes the way a girl starts," Alanna said. "But there are plenty of actresses who reach the top who aren't really beautiful. They have to have real talent, though, and a great deal of drive. I don't think I had much drive in the beginning. That developed later when I had a little taste of success. Now I do have drive and determination, and I know how important they are. And apparently I had the talent."

"If drive means wanting something terribly, I think I have it," I said.

"What do your father and mother say?"

Sooner or later, I knew she would have to ask that question. And there was no way around answering it honestly.

"They think I'm foolish. They think I'll get over it,

and they don't want a stage life for me at all. Or movies either."

Alanna was silent for a few moments, looking past me into the fire.

"Thank you for telling me," she said. "Some girls would have held that back."

I had nothing to say.

"Of course that makes it difficult, doesn't it?"

"That's why I wanted to talk to you," I said.

"H'm. But there's nothing I or anyone else can give you in the way of advice if your parents don't want this for you."

"They will when they understand," I told her urgently. "That's the whole thing. I've thought about doing other things before, and they just think this is going to pass the way they did. But it won't. It's what I want with all my heart, and if only they'd let me start, I could show them what I can do. Then they'd be proud of me. They'd stop worrying about my not having any talent and all that."

"Ah, talent," Alanna said. "You do have to have that, you know. It's never enough to just want to *be* something, or make someone proud of you. You have to have some sort of bent in the right direction in the beginning. You have to have something that can be developed, something that can grow. Something to work at. Do you have anything of the sort? Talent, I mean?"

"I don't know," I said. "I've been in only one school play, and I wasn't very good. But that doesn't prove anything. You said you weren't very good in the beginning either."

"I had something, just the same. It showed up in spite of me. I had to learn—that's true. But there was a basic talent there. It emerged when I gave myself a chance."

"So couldn't that be the case with me?"

"Perhaps. But you have loads of time to find out. If this feeling of yours lasts until you're in your twenties, or perhaps in your late teens, that is the time you can find out for sure."

I made a wailing sound of despair. "All those years! All that time ahead being nobody! I couldn't bear it!"

She smiled at me with a sort of loving sadness, so I knew that she liked me and wanted to help me. She *was* like the girls in her pictures. Steven was terribly wrong. I wondered why he had gone down such a wrong road about his own mother.

"Everybody is somebody," she said. "There aren't any nobodys. Every single person is unique and different and something in his own right. That's our search in life—to find out who we are. But it can take a very long time, and we can't all have what they call a career. It's more than that. A lot of us are still searching, even after we have a face we can present to the world."

"But I don't like what I am!"

"That *is* nonsense. You don't know who or what you are yet. That's what I'm trying to make you see."

"Steven doesn't like what he is either."

His mother was silent for a moment. "Steven is mistaken too. But he seems to have turned away from me lately. I can't talk to him anymore. I thought bringing you here might help a little, give him something new to think about. You're both going through a difficult phase, but there's plenty of time for you to find yourselves, if you'll just give yourselves a chance."

Time! That meant years of having nothing for anyone to be proud of. I couldn't worry about Steven just then.

"There isn't plenty of time!" I wailed. "There isn't! I thought you might help me. I thought—"

She sat up on the chaise longue and slid her feet to

the floor. "Come. I'd like to show you something," she said. "Come along with me."

I stopped my wailing, feeling a little silly, and let her take my hand. We went out of the room together and walked toward the stairs.

—8

Intruder in a Cabin

Alanna ran lightly up the stairs ahead of me and turned toward the rooms along the third-floor corridor. For just a moment I was afraid she might be taking me to her grandfather's studio full of sculptured figures. But it was before a room a door away that she stopped. I glanced ahead and saw that blank door of the figure room, with the key hanging on the hook outside it.

The other door was not locked. Alanna opened it and swept in ahead of me, flicking on the overhead light. There was less sun today, so this room was not flooded with daylight as that room down the hall had been. But it was not dim in the overhead light and I stood looking around in bewilderment.

For a moment or two I didn't realize what it was, or why she had brought me here. It was not a properly furnished room, but one into which all sorts of things had been piled. There was a dress dummy wearing a blue party gown that looked vaguely familiar. There was a wig mold on a table, with a hat set rakishly upon it. Along a shelf were pairs of shoes, and on the walls were hung a number of photographs in thin black frames.

The photographs were of Alanna. Some were of her head and shoulders; some were scenes from her motion pictures. I began to realize what the room must be. It was a collection of things from Alanna Graham's movies. I knew now why the blue dress was familiar. I had seen her wear that very gown in *Lilac Grove*.

My excitement grew. I ran over to the dress and touched it with careful fingers.

"I remember this," I said. "You wore it when you danced in the very last scene."

Alanna looked pleased and her eyes were a little misty. "Yes! I loved the making of that picture. I felt sad when we were through. We had such fun and we were all such good friends. It isn't always like that. Sometimes there are actors who don't like each other, or a director who's hard to work with. But for *Lilac Grove* everything went beautifully. Look here, Jan— do you remember this?"

A teddy bear sat on a shelf, his button eyes slightly crossed, his grin appealing.

"Of course!" I cried. "He was in *Sunrise Farm* when you went to the carnival with Jake. And you won Teddy by throwing a ball. I do remember."

On the wall above the bear's head was a framed scene from the picture, with Jake and Alanna singing to each other. What a wonderful room this was. I began to run from one object to the next, while Alanna watched me with a pleased look on her face. I remembered so much. I was a real fan, and she knew it.

When I'd seen as much as I could, I whirled about in the middle of the floor and flung out my arms.

"What a wonderful, marvelous room!"

"It isn't anything yet," Alanna said. "I had everything shipped here where there was space for it, and I've just unpacked these things and set them around. But when I feel like it, I'd like to come up here and arrange everything nicely. Make a real display room out of it."

I remembered something. "When Steven brought me

up here the other day he pointed to this door and said this was his very favorite room in the house."

She looked as if I had given her an unexpected present. "Did he really? But he doesn't seem to like my pictures lately, and he's changed about so many things. I don't know——" She broke off, and I knew she didn't want to talk about this with me. But I was right. She loved Steven a great deal and there wasn't any matter of not being proud of him. He had somehow got mixed up in his thinking, so that he had gone off down a wrong road that was making him bad-tempered and unhappy. I wondered why. But this was here and now, and I couldn't worry about Steven while I was in this marvelous place.

"I'd give anything to be famous and have a room like this," I said.

Alanna laughed softly. "Being famous is something that comes out of a lot of hard work and dedication. I've wanted to collect a few things from every one of my pictures, and there isn't an item in this room that wasn't worked for with blood, sweat, and tears. That pair of shoes—the green ones over there. There was always something wrong with them and they hurt my feet. I wore them in a scene that I had to play over and over—with my feet killing me, and not a bit of it being allowed to show in my face. I'm a pro, you know. That means I'm a professional, and I don't fuss about things. I do what has to be done and accept that as part of my job. It means everything to me now. It's the sort of life I want to lead more than anything else." She touched the blue dress and her tone grew suddenly tense. "More than anything else! I couldn't give it up. I couldn't!"

"But you don't need to, do you?" I said, puzzled by her intensity.

"Sometimes it's hard to live up to what people expect of me. I'm not really all the things the public thinks I am. That girl's a make-believe character."

This was what Steven had said, but he had seemed to mean it in an uglier way.

"I don't think that matters," I told her. "It doesn't matter, does it, if people think you're like your pictures? *I* think you're like that."

Her face softened and there was a shine of tears in her eyes. "Thank you, dear Jan. But how would you feel if I proved not to be what you think me at all? Could you forgive me for that?"

"I don't think there'd be anything to forgive."

She bent her dark head and rested her forehead against the shoulder of the blue dress. "Nobody has idols anymore in the movies. I'm one of the very few left. They've made a sort of legend of me, and all sorts of people who miss having idols flock to my pictures. They're family pictures and the people who go to them would all turn against me in a moment if everything came crashing down."

"But why should it crash down?"

"That's right, why should it?" She raised her head and when she looked at me again her face had changed. All the softness, the gentleness had gone from it and she looked hard and angry. "It's not going to!"

The change in her didn't change me. I still thought she was wonderful. But what she had achieved all seemed to lie so far ahead for me—if ever. And I wanted to do something, *be* somebody right now. I couldn't understand what she was worried about, and I was worried about me.

As she moved toward the door, she was gentle again. She seemed to understand what I was feeling.

"It always takes so long to grow up, Jan. At least it seems that way. But it happens before you know it. Before you know it, you'll be looking back and wondering where the years went."

That didn't seem possible now. "Thank you for showing me," I said softly. If she had been my idol before, now she was my idol more than ever. I didn't want to remember the other things she had said.

"I'll take you back to Steven," she said. "I'll be very glad if you can be friends. He needs someone his own age around. Even if you're here only for a couple of weeks. The next time you come be sure to bring your brother."

I thought of telling her about Harry Mercer and the lie he had told, the way he had tried to prevent my coming that day. But I didn't want to worry her and spoil the nice feeling that lay between us. As we went toward the stairs, I asked her something I had in my mind.

"Is there any way you can tell about talent? I mean—" but I didn't know how to put it into words so it wouldn't sound silly and too ambitious.

"Perhaps." She looked at me brightly. "You might read me something, or play a little part. And it wouldn't mean a great deal if it didn't turn out well."

"But if it did turn out well?"

"That might mean a little something. And I don't think your parents would mind our trying."

I felt suddenly hopeful. "Then will you let me try?"

She regarded me soberly. "Perhaps I'll make a bargain with you. Perhaps we can draw Steven into this. Involve him. He reads rather well, so maybe you can persuade him to help you. Practice a scene with him first. He's written some little plays himself. It would be something for you to do together. And you can play a scene for me. It might help—everything."

I couldn't see Steven doing anything that didn't please him, and I thought it unlikely that he would help me. Yet I knew that if this was the only way she'd give me a chance, I had to try. But before I could tell her that I would, a querulous voice called to her from the open door of a room down the hall. Grandfather Burton's voice.

"Alanna? Is that you? I want to talk to you, Alanna."

"Yes, of course, Grandfather," she said. And to me. "Come with me. He likes company. I believe you met him the other day, didn't you?"

We walked down the hall to the big, darkened room and went inside. Cousin Daphne wasn't there and the old man sat against his pillows, looking lonely.

This time I didn't go close enough for him to grasp me by the wrist but stayed out in the middle of the room. Alanna went to the bed and asked him if he wanted anything, and he said, "Only to talk."

"We might as well sit down for a few minutes," Alanna said to me, so we took chairs near the bed. "What do you want to talk about, Grandfather?"

"Steven," he said. "I want to talk about Steven."

"What about Steven?" Alanna sounded uneasy.

"What's the matter with the boy?"

"Matter with him, Grandfather? I don't understand."

The old man wriggled disapprovingly under his covers, "Oh, I think you do. Something's bothering him. He's changed. He scowls all the time, and he doesn't want to come upstairs to read to me anymore."

Alanna gave me a helpless look. "It's just a mood, I think. Growing boys have moods, Grandfather."

"He behaves as though he didn't like you anymore, Alanna. Is there mother and son trouble between you these days?"

"Perhaps. A little. I'm not sure what the trouble is."

"Well, don't let it go on. Find out what's wrong. When you let children drift away from you, they get into trouble. You got into trouble, didn't you, Alanna? After you ran away from home and left your grandmother and me so unkindly. You needn't have done that, dear. We suffered, you know."

"I know. I'm sorry. But that's all a long time ago. It doesn't matter anymore, Grandfather. I'm back home with you now for a good long visit, and we want to forget all that old unhappiness. Jan here doesn't know anything about it. So let's not talk about it, Grandfather. I'll try to have a talk with Steven soon. I've been meaning to. I want to know what's troubling him."

He reached out a thin hand in Alanna's direction. "That's my good girl. We can't have things go wrong with Steven. That won't do, will it?" Then he turned abruptly to me. "You—little girl. Come back to see me sometime. I'd like to talk to you."

I didn't know what to say, but Alanna took his hand and bent to kiss him. Then she gestured me quietly toward the door. "We'll have another talk before long, Grandfather. Jan has to go home soon, and I want her to have a little more time with Steven."

We went out of the room together and were just in time to see Steven running down the hall toward the back of the house with a pair of binoculars in his hands. He didn't see us, but let himself through a door where the hallway ended.

"Now what's he up to?" Alanna murmured. "Let's go and see." But before we turned to follow Steven, she put a hand on my arm. "Don't say anything to Steven about what Grandfather just said. It might upset him. Grandfather is getting very old, and he's trapped up here in his room all alone and unable to move about. So he broods over all sorts of things. Daphne tries to help, but she doesn't always behave cheerfully, and I think her presence bothers him sometimes."

Of course I wouldn't have mentioned any of this to Steven, but I found myself pondering old Mr. Oliver's words about Alanna getting into trouble when she was young. She had quieted him quickly, so I couldn't tell what he had meant.

Steven had closed the door at the end of the hall, but Alanna opened it and went through, with me after her. It let us into a room that was bare of furniture, although two opened screens stood along one wall.

Steven had crossed the bare floor to push open shutters and was leaning on the sill with the binoculars to his eyes.

Alanna smiled and nodded. "I know what it is," she whispered. "He's fascinated by an old cabin on our property. This is the only window you can see it from."

I knew about the cabin, though I hadn't realized it was on the Oliver property. Mike and I had discovered it several years ago in our wanderings about the area. It might once have served as a small summer place for people who came out from the city. Mike and I had explored it several times and even had had some picnics there.

"What do you see?" Alanna asked as she moved toward Steven.

Obviously he hadn't heard us come in, and he swung around startled, looking almost guilty for some reason. He frowned at his mother and me and turned back to looking through the glasses.

"Is something interesting going on?" Alanna asked.

He shifted the glasses a little, as if he followed some movement. "I can't tell who it is. It's too far away. But I can see the cabin, and somebody just went in the door."

"Let me see," Alanna held out her hand for the glasses and he gave them up reluctantly.

She focused them on the distant cabin, which I could make out as a faraway blur of brown among evergreen trees. But after a moment she gave them back to Steven and he focused them again.

"I couldn't see anyone," she said. "And anyway, does it matter?"

"Whoever is there is trespassing," Steven said. "He hasn't any right to go in."

"Oh, pooh!" Alanna said lightly. "The cabin is just standing there deserted, and I suppose strangers wander upon it now and then. It's right on the trail that comes down from the top of the mountain. No harm is done if someone looks into it once in a while."

Steven kept on staring, and after a moment he stiffened. "There—he's come out again. He's going away down the trail around a corner of the cabin. But I can't see his face or tell what he looks like."

"Well, don't worry about it," Alanna said. "I suppose I ought to get Grandfather to have the old place torn down. Then it won't tempt anyone to trespass."

"No!" Steven cried sharply. "No—I don't want it torn down. You said it could be mine whenever I stayed here. I like having a cabin in the woods. I go there lots of times."

"All right—we won't have it torn down," his mother said soothingly. "But now I was just about to bring Jan back to you. I thought you might like to walk her up to her house before it gets dark."

"Okay, I'll take her home," he said without enthusiasm. "At least I can get her through the front door so she won't break anything else."

We had started along the hall toward the stairs. For a little while I'd forgotten about the Greek jar. Now I remembered that I must say something more to Alanna about it.

"My father will pay for it," I told her quickly. "I know it must have cost an awful lot of money, and I'm terribly sorry. Steven said it was your favorite piece, and—"

"It's not," she said carelessly. "Steven likes to worry people sometimes. Please don't fret about it. Accidents happen. I've broken things myself—other people's things."

I wondered if Steven would mention the picture I had found among the broken pieces, but he said nothing, and when we reached his room again I couldn't see the brown envelope anywhere around.

Steven took me home shortly and had very little to say on the way. I tried to bring up the subject of playing a part for Alanna with his help, but it was apparently the wrong time for asking, because he didn't pay much attention to me. He just made a snorting sound that dismissed the whole idea. He seemed to be lost in his own faraway thoughts, and I wondered if they had anything to do with that cabin in the woods. Anyway, I would just have to try again to persuade Steven to help me.

—9

The Cabin

The very next morning Mike suggested a visit to the cabin. It was something different to do, and we usually went there once or twice on every visit to Gramp's.

"I've just found out that it's on Oliver property," I told him. "Steven was watching it through binoculars yesterday and he said somebody went into it. He said the man was trespassing. But Alanna didn't seem to care."

"We've always gone there, and we don't hurt anything," Mike said doggedly.

I was willing enough to go. Steven's behavior had made me curious—not just about who was visiting the cabin, but about why Steven himself was so interested.

Gram had some chores for us, so we didn't get to go until after lunch. Then we walked along the snow-rutted road that ended a little way past Gramp's house and turned into the woods. We wound through evergreens, following a path that bore foot tracks going and coming, as though more than one person had gone back and forth over the path—or one person several times. There seemed to be a man's prints, and the smaller prints of a boy. Steven's? I wondered.

Snow had melted around the cabin, so it wasn't possible to tell whether the tracks followed the branch path up the mountain, or actually went to the cabin door.

When we neared the small building, Mike grew cautious.

"Let's have a look in the windows first," he said.

I was glad enough not to go barging right in after Steven's strange behavior yesterday. The cabin had only two rooms—one the living section up in front, the other a smaller kitchen area at the back. He went to the living area windows first and peered in.

The room was furnished with a few old sticks of furniture and there was an empty fireplace with a bench drawn before it. No one was there. We slipped back to the kitchen windows and looked in. This time we could see that someone was in the room.

Steven stood on a wooden stool, reaching up toward a high cupboard. He looked tall up there with his black hair in the shadow of the cupboard door. We couldn't tell what he was doing, but Mike nudged me around toward the front of the cabin.

"Let's go in," he said.

We went in quietly and Steven didn't hear us. When Mike opened the door between the kitchen and the living room, he was still on the stool, reaching high, his back toward us. We couldn't see what was in the cupboard, but when he brought his hand down it held a key. Just before he jumped to the floor from the stool, he saw us and the familiar scowl came over his face, spoiling his good looks.

"Hello," Mike said. "Is this your cabin?"

The key had vanished into his pocket, the cupboard doors were closed. "It belongs to my grandfather," he said. "So you're—"

"Trespassing!" I broke in. "But your mother doesn't seem to care who comes here, and we've always visited the cabin other years when we've been at Gramp's."

"You're not supposed to come here," Steven said gruffly. "I wish Mother would lock it up. But she thinks it would only be broken into, so it's better to leave it standing open."

"Do you really care if we picnic here?" I asked.

Steven turned his scowl on me. "Somebody else has been here—picnicking," he said, not answering my question. "Somebody built a fire in the wood stove and heated a can of beans."

"A tramp, maybe?" I said.

"I don't think we have tramps around here." Steven shook his head. "It must have been the same man I saw through my glasses yesterday."

"Has he done any harm?" Mike asked.

Again Steven shook his head, though reluctantly. "I guess not."

We all refrained from saying anything about what Steven had been doing with a key back in that kitchen cupboard, but I knew Mike was as curious as I, and we didn't care for it when Steven gave us each a little shove toward the door when he prepared to leave.

"We thought we'd stay awhile," Mike said.

"You don't have permission," Steven said rudely. "Come along out."

So we had to leave with Steven, whether we wanted to or not. But on the path toward home he hurried ahead and soon left us behind. When he was out of sight, apparently trusting us to follow, Mike tugged at my elbow. There was a mischievous light in his eyes.

"Let's go back," he said.

We turned on the path and ran lightly toward the cabin. Steven didn't follow us, and we reached the door breathless and laughing. This was one up on Steven, whose high-handed manner Mike hadn't liked any better than I did.

It took us no time to run through the living area to the kitchen, and Mike climbed onto the stool where Steven had stood. When he opened the cupboard doors we saw just one object sitting on the top shelf. It was a gray steel box with a metal handle for carrying. It had been pushed far to the back, but when Mike pulled it out, he quickly found that it was locked. That was the key Steven had put in his pocket, undoubtedly.

"Push it back again," I said to Mike, and he slid the box into the dark corner where Steven had left it.

This was just one more mystery connected with the Oliver house. Why had Steven Nelson brought a lockbox here to hide in an empty cabin? Probably it was the presence of the box that had troubled him yesterday and made him worry about the man who had come into the cabin. And he had come over here today to make sure the box had not been disturbed. But if he had hidden some treasure in it, why wouldn't he keep it at the big house? Why would he hide it away in a cabin in the woods?

Just as we had closed the cupboard doors and were about to leave, we heard a sound at the front of the cabin. The door opened softly, then closed, and steps sounded on the wooden floor. I clutched at Mike and we stood together in silence. If Steven had come back, he was going to be angry with us, and I knew he was in the right and we were in the wrong. Now we really were trespassing. But for a moment nothing more happened.

Whoever was in the next room was setting something down—something heavy that clunked. Mike and I stood very still. After a moment of more walking around, the steps came toward the door between the two rooms, and it was pulled open. We found ourselves staring in surprise at Joe Reed.

He stared back at us, equally surprised, and finally managed a questioning, "Hello?"

"Hello," Mike said. "What are you doing here?"

"I might ask you the same thing." Joe looked solemn, as he always did, but I thought he was a little worried too. His sandy head was bare. His thick hair had been ruffled by the wind, and his thin face looked pinched by the cold.

"We asked first," I said.

He managed a faint grin. "I just found this place a few days ago. I had myself a picnic here one day. Today I brought over some supplies I thought I'd keep here, just in case."

Just in case what? I wondered. I saw that the heavy thing he had set down was a carton containing some canned items, as well as instant coffee, powdered milk, and so on.

"Why would you want to picnic here?" I asked. "You've got your own place back at Gramp's."

"Just for a change," he said. "Now it's your turn. What are you doing here?"

"We always come here," Mike said. "We like it here and sometimes we've used it for a picnic too. But Steven Nelson was here just now and he says the cabin is on Oliver property and we're all trespassing."

"The boy comes here?" Joe asked.

I nodded. "He says it's his cabin and he likes to come here. I expect we'd all better go before he comes back and finds us."

Joe seemed to accept that as a good idea, but first he picked up his carton of provisions and carried it into the kitchen. He opened a different cupboard door from the one that hid the lockbox and shoved the carton onto a shelf. Then he closed the door.

"I'll leave this stuff here," he said. And added again, "Just in case."

After that we started back to the house, walking single file through the woods. Joe Reed seemed to have nothing more to say and we didn't talk at all. I had a feeling that he hadn't been pleased to find us there or to have us know that he was stocking the cabin with provisions. I couldn't help wondering what he was up to and why on earth he would want to do a thing like that.

But when we got back to the house we forgot all about the cabin and Joe Reed, because Gram was ill. She was in severe pain, and Gramp was worried to pieces.

He came to the door while we were walking up the drive and beckoned us all into the house, including Joe.

"I'll have to take her to the hospital," he said. "I may have to stay there, and I don't know what to do about you children. I don't want to leave you alone in the house, but—" he broke off helplessly.

I ran to Gram where she lay on the living room couch, looking pale and ill. I bent to kiss her cheek and she smiled at me faintly, not looking like her usual strong and dignified self.

"I know!" I said to Gramp. "We could stay with Alanna."

He stared at me. "But we scarcely know this lady, and—"

"I'm sure it would be all right," I said eagerly. "She's awfully nice and she would understand that this is an emergency. Why don't you call her on the phone, Gramp?"

Joe Reed said, "Is there anything I can do?"

"You'll have to look after things while I'm gone," Gramp said, but I could tell that he was reluctant to leave us in Joe's charge. I urged Alanna upon him again, and after a moment he went to the phone and called her up.

We followed him into the hall to listen and heard him tell her about Gram's illness and the problem that faced us. We could hear Alanna's voice sounding enthusiastic on the phone, though we couldn't make out her words. But it was easy to tell by Gramp's air of relief that Alanna was agreeing readily.

"She's coming for you in her car," Gramp said when he put the phone down. "She says to pack some clothes and she'll pick you up in fifteen or twenty minutes. She was very kind and understanding and she says it will be no trouble at all, with their big house. So do everything you can to help and don't make yourselves nuisances."

He went to pack a small bag for Gram, and Mike and I hurried upstairs. Joe had gone outdoors. I put something together in a hurry, feeling worried about Gram, yet excited about a chance to stay at the big house. Now I'd surely be able to talk to Steven and we'd get to read something for Alanna. We all met quickly downstairs and Alanna drove up in her car before Gramp left for the hospital.

She was more efficient than I'd have expected her to be. She supported Gram on one side to get her out to the car and helped to bed her down in the back seat. Mike and I ran around carrying Gram's things, but Joe never showed up at all. He stayed out of sight in his room, and I wondered if he'd been offended because Gramp hadn't wanted to leave us in his charge.

Before Gramp left, he went out to give Joe instructions and then came back to lock up the house. When he drove off, Alanna smiled at us happily.

"How lovely to have houseguests for a few days. Though I'm sorry about the reason. I told Steven and I know he'll be pleased."

I noticed she didn't say he *was* pleased. We picked up our bags and got into the back seat of Alanna's car, and she drove us through the woods to her house. Cousin Daphne came to let us in the door, looking anything but happy.

"We have overnight guests," Alanna told her. "Perhaps guests for a few days. I think we can give them each a bedroom on the second floor."

Before Cousin Daphne could answer we heard sounds

on the stairs. When I looked around I saw one of the maids running down, looking frightened and upset.

Cousin Daphne turned from us at once. "Is something wrong?"

"You told me to dust the sculptures in the studio, and I just went in there. The figures have been moving around. I always thought they could move—I always thought that at night—"

"Hush!" Cousin Daphne said. "Don't talk such nonsense."

Alanna went over to the girl. "What is it, Marie? You know those figures don't shift about by themselves. Has someone been moving them?"

The girl was really frightened. Her teeth were chattering so she could hardly talk. "Wh-wh-who would m-m-move them?"

"Let's go and see," Alanna said.

She and Cousin Daphne started up the stairs and I pulled Mike after them, because I didn't want to miss whatever was going on. We followed the others up to the third floor and down the hall to the studio, where the door stood open, the key in the lock. Alanna swept ahead of us into the room. The maid stayed close to her, shivering and Cousin Daphne moving more slowly, walked into the room behind Alanna. Mike and I stood in the doorway.

So far as I could tell, everything looked the same as always, with those weird stone figures standing all around. Some of the smaller ones rested on pedestals, while larger ones stood on the floor. Some were twisted this way and that, with a woman's figure near me looking over her shoulder in frightened fashion as if something were pursuing her. The look on her face made me cast a quick glance over my own shoulder.

All the dust covers had been left off since Steven had removed them, and Alanna moved about, touching a figure here and there, studying them. "Yes, you're right. Someone has changed the position of several figures in the room. They're easily moved. It wouldn't be hard to do. Do you know anything about this, Daphne?"

Cousin Daphne was shaking her head gloomily. "They were all as usual when I was in here yesterday. I noticed they were dusty and I sent Marie in here for a good cleaning today."

"I'll speak to Steven," Alanna said. "Perhaps he was being mischievous."

But Steven had heard us and he came down the hall to see what was happening. "I haven't moved those beastly old things," he said. "I haven't been in this room since the other day when I showed it to Mike and Jan."

I had a creepy feeling up my spine. Unless someone was lying, that left only Mr. Mercer, and it didn't seem very likely that he would come up here and start moving things about.

Alanna didn't seem to think so either, and she looked at Steven reproachfully, as though she still suspected mischief on his part.

"Anyway, they should be dusted, Marie," she said. "So you'd better do as Mrs. Price has suggested. Don't worry about their positions being changed, since it really doesn't matter how they stand. I'll see if I can find out more about this later."

I think Marie didn't like being left alone with her dusting in that room, but she made no further objection when we went away and left her to her room of monsters.

Alanna presented us to Steven as visitors and he looked neither pleased nor displeased.

"Mike can have the room next to mine," he said.

So that was the way we worked it out on the second floor. That left the room on the other side of Mike's for me, and Alanna took me along the second-floor hallway and showed me into it. I found it a pleasant room, with maple furniture and bright chintz draperies at the two windows. Both looked out toward the hillside. I could see Gramp's house high above us, which gave me a comfortable feeling of being close to home. They left me there to get settled, so I unpacked the things I'd brought with me and hung my clothes in the closet. Then I looked into the hall.

That was when I began counting doors. I remembered very well the way the doors ran upstairs. Mike's room was underneath Alanna's room of movie treasures. My room—and there wasn't any mistake—was directly underneath the room that had been Burton Oliver's studio. The monster room, as I was beginning to call it in my own mind. That gave me an uneasy feeling, and I wondered what I would do if I woke up in the middle of the night and heard something moving around up there.

I could hear someone now. That would be Marie, busy at her cleaning, but that was different. I tried to shrug off my feeling and get back to being happy over coming here, but a little edge was gone from my earlier pleasure. And I thought about Gram and was sad.

For the rest of the afternoon Steven made himself reasonably agreeable. We played games in his room and looked at some of his things. He and Mike both had good stamp collections and could talk about stamps, while I enjoyed looking through his books. I found one I'd been wanting to read and he said I could take it with me when I went to my room. All the while I waited for the right moment to ask him about helping me read for Alanna from one of his plays. This time when I asked him I wanted to have his full attention. And I wanted to talk to him alone. But the right moment just didn't offer itself.

Late in the afternoon Gramp phoned from the hospital and talked to Mike. Gram was feeling better, but she would have to stay for a few days while tests were being made. It looked as though we might have to stay at Alanna's over Christmas. Gramp had taken a room in a hotel in town, and he would remain with Gram at the hospital most of the time. At least Gram was more comfortable now, and that was a relief. But I felt worried and disappointed. I didn't think I wanted to stay at Alanna's longer than to accomplish my purpose.

Dinner that night was served in the big, dark dining room downstairs. Wood paneling ran up all the walls, contributing to the dark effect, and the wallpaper above it was a dark wine red. The furniture was large and heavy and old-fashioned, and the pictures seemed to be dark, wild scenes of storms on land and sea. A big crystal chandelier hung over the table, but it didn't seem to lend the room much light.

Alanna sat at one end of the table and Mr. Mercer at the other, with Cousin Daphne and Steven across from each other. I sat beside Steven, and Mike sat next to Cousin Daphne. Alanna did her best to make it a cheerful meal, but I'm afraid she didn't have much help. Daphne Price was naturally gloomy, and Harry Mercer was busy with his food, though perhaps he talked more than the rest of us. Steven said very little. He was still peeved with his mother about something —perhaps her accusation about that room upstairs. And Mike and I were subdued by our surroundings and by being with strangers, so we didn't exactly bubble. I already missed the talkative meals we had with Gramp and Gram, with Gramp often holding forth at length and the rest of us interrupting to make contributions of our own.

At least they had a good cook—the roast beef and browned potatoes were delicious. And so was my favorite apple-and-celery salad with nuts. We had ice cream and cookies for dessert, and there was plenty of everything, so we weren't a bit hungry by the time we left the table.

Afterward we all went into the huge drawing droom and gathered for a while around the fire. Strangely, there was more easy conversation now. Mr. Mercer talked about Hollywood and told some stories, and Cousin Daphne asked questions about life in California. Along the way she said something that surprised me.

"You know, I always meant to be an actress," she said. "But I didn't have the opportunities that came Alanna's way."

"I made my own opportunities," Alanna said, and I thought her voice sounded grim.

Somehow I didn't care much for the fact that Cousin Daphne, like me, had wanted to be an actress. I certainly didn't want to turn out like her in the end— disappointed and gloomy.

As I listened to all this I began to feel a little sorry for Steven. Apparently he had never known family life like our own when Mother and Dad were home, or like the life we had with Gramp and Gram. I wondered if he had a happier life out on the Coast when his mother was working on a picture and lived there.

After a while Steven left his place and came over to where Mike and I sat together at one end of the couch.

"Do you want me to show you something I'm making?" he asked us in a low voice.

Anything was better than this stiff, not very happy grown-up world. So when he told his mother he was going upstairs, we went with him.

First he put Thor outside for the night, and then he led the way upstairs. "This is a secret," he said. "You're not to tell anybody."

—10

A Tapping on the Window

Steven took us up to the room at the end of the house where he had gone when he looked at the cabin through his binoculars. I'd noticed then that there were screens in the room, though I hadn't looked behind them. Now he switched on an overhead light, folded back the two screens, and leaned them against a wall.

Behind the screens, tacked along one wall, was a long strip of drawing paper, torn from a roll. It had been partly filled with colored pictures.

"It's going to be a mural," Steven said. "For my mother to hang in her movie room." He looked almost shy about showing us his work, and I felt a surge of warmth toward him.

It was easy to recognize what he had done. Each segment of the paper, except for empty sections at the very beginning and at the end, carried a scene from one of Alanna's pictures. The section he was working on now was *Lilac Grove* and I recognized Alanna's blue dress as she ran among the children.

"They're awfully good," I said.

He had put an enormous amount of work into the strip of pictures, with all sorts of small detail imaginatively painted—things anyone would remember from her films, but things Alanna especially would recognize and enjoy. I felt pleased with him for a change. I could see the love that had gone into the work and how it would eventually make up for his scowls and make everything right between his mother and him.

Mike added his own words of praise, though he wasn't an Alanna Graham fan the way I was, and the pictures couldn't mean as much to him as far as recognition went. But he appreciated Steven's real talent in drawing. Those pictures were *good.* I thought wistfully to myself that here was someone else with talent, while I—but this was not the time to worry about me, and I hoped Steven was enjoying our praise.

"Your mother will be awfully pleased," I said.

At once Steven scowled again. "Oh, no, she won't! She'll be mad when I get it done. That is, she will if I finish it up the way I think I will."

"How do you mean?" I asked.

He waved a hand toward the empty spaces at the beginning of the strip. "I don't think she'll like what I put in there. It won't match up with all the rest. I hope it hurts her. I hope—" He broke off angrily and brought the screens to unfold and spread before the drawings again.

"I guess I'll go to bed," he said crossly. Then he seemed to remember that to some extent he was our host tonight. "Is there anything you want?" he asked us.

"Only the book from your room," I said.

He let me get the book, and then, even though it was still early, Mike and I went down the hall to our rooms. I stopped in Mike's doorway for a moment, after Steven had left us.

"My room's right under the mons—that is, it's under the studio. You wouldn't want to switch, would you?"

"I don't think we'd better," Mike said. "We've been put where they want us. And what difference does it make, anyway? Your monsters aren't going to come through the ceiling."

He made me feel silly. "Just the same, I don't want to wake up and hear them moving around up there."

Mike only grinned and I went on to my own room. It was a very pleasant room and it even had a reading light beside the bed, which is my favorite luxury. When I'd had a bath in the bathroom across the hall and was in my pajamas, I curled up in bed, with the light beside me, and began to read Steven's book. It was an adventure-mystery story, and quite exciting. It kept my mind off the room overhead, for which I was thankful.

When I was getting sleepy and was just about ready to put the book aside and slip down under the covers, a light tap sounded on my door.

I called, "Come in," and Alanna came into the room.

She looked very pretty in the green dress she had worn at dinner, and she was smiling as she crossed the room to me.

"It's been ages since I've had so many young people to say good night to," she told me. "Out in California, Steven has friends stay overnight sometimes. But there's been no one around here that he has grown friendly with. What book are you reading? Oh, that's a good one. Steven liked it. May I tuck you in, Jan?"

I put the book on the bed table and slid down under the covers. She pulled them up to my chin and leaned over to kiss me lightly on the cheek. She smelled a little like lilacs, and it was very special to have Alanna Graham kiss me good night. But before she could reach for the light, I stopped her. With night pressing against the windows, the dark trees all around —and that room upstairs—I had to ask a question, no matter how foolish.

"Those figures in the studio don't really move around by themselves, do they?"

She caught her breath at my words and then tried to laugh. Somehow the sound didn't ring quite true. "Oh, you mustn't listen to that silly Marie. She's probably heard those old stories in the village. And there's nothing true about them. Of course sculptured figures can't move. I still think it was Steven who was up to his usual mischief. I don't know what's got into him lately."

"What old stories?" I asked.

"Oh, nothing, really. There are always stories about an old house like this, but they must have died out by now."

"Stories about Burton Oliver's sculptures?" I pressed her.

"I don't want to talk about it, Jan. There's nothing to worry you about that room. Truly. I'll turn out the light now, and you can go to sleep. If you like, I'll leave your door ajar, so you'll get a sliver of light from the hall. Light helps sometimes when you're in a strange house for the first night."

I didn't say anything more, and she went quietly away, leaving the door open a crack. I lay there watching the band of light and trying not to think about that upstairs room. After a while I drowsed off in spite of myself and I must have slept for a long while.

The thing that wakened me was a sound from the room above. Something thumped on the floor—as if one of those figures had taken a clumping step. I lay awake on my pillow with my heart bumping raggedly and all my senses alert. I lay absolutely still, listening with all of me. There was no further noise, and I began to think I must have dreamed what I'd heard. My eyelids grew heavy again and I was just drowsing off when I heard a different sound. A familiar sliding sound like a window opening, though I was too sleepy to

identify it right away. Now I knew something was going on in that room upstairs.

Next came a tapping at my window, and that froze
me beneath my covers for a long moment. Then the
tapping came again, as though something swung
against the glass. This time it was like a summons—a
hard tap-tapping that seemed to call me to the window.
In spite of my fright, I had to see what was happening.
I wasn't so foolish as to think that one of those stone
figures had climbed down to my window ledge.

I slipped out of bed and turned on a light. All was
quiet overhead. I went to one of my windows and
looked out. Something was swinging against the glass.
It tapped and swung away, tapped and swung away.
With hands that had begun to perspire, I thrust the
window up and looked out at the small conical object
that seemed to float suspended in space. As I stared,
it swung toward me and I reached out a hand and
caught it. My fingers closed over a smooth, solid surface. The object must have been suspended on a thread
because when I clasped it there was a momentary taut-
ness of resistance. Then something snapped and the
thing came loose in my hand. I brought it into my
room.

What I held in my hand was a fair-sized shell of
the cone variety. It was cream-colored, with a brown
scattering of spots all over it. I set it down on the bed
and closed the window. Even though I was wide awake
now, I couldn't understand what had happened. Why
should this shell have been let down from the room
above and allowed to swing against my windowpane?
Was it Steven being mischievous, wanting to torment
me?

Now that I was wide awake, I didn't want to stay
here alone, trying to figure out the mystery. I put on
my robe and went into the hall. The time must have
been well into the middle of the night because though

the bracket lamps burned dimly in the hall, the house was still and the stairs were dark and empty. I didn't want to waken everyone, so I went to Mike's door, which hadn't been left open for the light, and I turned the knob softly, whispering into the opening.

"Mike, are you asleep?"

He grunted and turned over in his bed. I stepped into his room and closed the door behind me.

"Turn on a light," I whispered. "I have to talk to you, Mike."

He came awake at last. I heard the bed creak in the darkness as he sat up and reached for a light. A moment later there was a glow from the lamp on his bed table, and it showed me Mike staring at me sleepily.

"What do you want?" he said. "What's the matter?"

I carried the shell to the bedside and held it out to him. "Someone came into the monster room and and opened a window and let down this shell to tap on my window. I think it was on a thread that broke when I took hold of it."

Mike took the shell from me and turned it over in his hands. Then he gave it back, as mystified as I but wider awake now.

"It must be Steven," he said. "Nobody else would do a thing like that. Is his door closed?"

Mike came with me as we looked into the hall. Steven's door was blank and closed. When Mike had found slippers to put on, he beckoned me into the hall.

"Let's go upstairs and see," he whispered.

I didn't want to go near that overhead room, but Mike was already marching toward the upper stairs, his pajamas flashing blue in the dim light, and there was nothing to do but follow him. The stairs were drafty and chill, with only a light on the floor above to pull us on. I suppose anyone who belonged to the house would know where to light the stairs, but we stumbled upward through gloom.

Mike moved quickly ahead of me and paid no attention to my soft gasp of protest when he started toward the room above mine. The door of Alanna's movie collection was closed. Old Mr. Burton Oliver's door was open down at the other end of the hall, and so was the door of another room. Probably Cousin Daphne's. But all was silent down the hall, and Mike and I moved softly in the opposite direction.

The studio door was locked, and the key hung in its place. Mike took it down and slipped it into the lock. It made a slight grating sound. I held my breath. Nothing stirred in the hallway or in any of the rooms. Quietly Mike thrust open the door and I stood very close to him, so I could grab him if I had to. He wasn't afraid at all, but I felt terrified of this room in the dark.

It was not completely black, though, because moonlight came through Burton Oliver's skylight. Perhaps that made everything worse, since the moon was bright and it cast shadows among the dim figures, multiplying them. I clutched at the back of Mike's pajamas and tried not to see anything on either side as I followed him toward the window. We could tell at once that it was still open, with cold winter air blowing in.

"Somebody was here," Mike whispered over his shoulder. "He didn't stop to close the window after you took the shell." He felt along the windowsill with his hands and a moment later he pulled something in. "You were right about the thread, Jan. He left it on the sill."

Mike reached out toward me and I felt the silky strand of thread across my wrist. Something clattered on the floor and Mike bent to pick up the spool that was still attached to the long, unwound piece of thread. He gave it to me and I began absently to wind up the thread that had reached all the way down to my window. As quietly as he could, Mike shoved the window down and turned toward the room.

Suddenly all the figures in that moon-silvered place seemed to come alive and move in their own thick shadows. I clutched at Mike a bit wildly.

"I can't go through them again. I can't! If one of them touches me, I'll scream!"

"Don't be an idiot!" Mike said crossly. "And do be quiet."

The girl with the baby dragon in her hand, and the sly, wicked face, seemed to reach toward me, and I gasped and hung on to Mike.

"If you choke me, I can't move," he said. "And you've got to be quiet."

But it was already too late for that. My last cry had been too loud, and I heard someone coming down the hall. A moment later a hand reached in to touch the light switch and the light overhead came on. Cousin Daphne, wrapped in a long brown robe, stood in the doorway looking at us in astonishment.

"What are you doing here?" she asked softly, clearly not wanting to wake the rest of the house. "You both belong downstairs."

I nudged Mike, because quite suddenly I didn't want to say anything about the shell. "I thought I heard something moving in this room," I said. "So I got Mike and we came upstairs to see."

The woman threw an uncertain glance around the room, and Mike took up the story.

"Someone *was* here. A window was open. I just closed it because it was letting cold into the house." He said nothing about the shell, so I knew he had understood my nudge.

Cousin Daphne went across to the window and tried it. Then she shivered and made a shooing motion at us with both hands.

"Go back to your rooms, children. I'm sure Alanna wouldn't approve of your wandering around the house at night."

With the light on, it was easier to cross the figure-thronged room, but even then I brushed against a hunter with an outstretched bow and gave a little squeal, as though he had touched me deliberately.

"Hush!" Cousin Daphine said. "We mustn't wake Grandfather Burton or he'll be up for hours. And I need my sleep. All I do is tend that old man."

In the hall it was Cousin Daphne who locked the door and hung up the key. Then she gave us each a little push.

"Hurry now. I'll light the stairs for you. And don't get up again. Or if you must, call me and I'll see if there's anything wrong."

Mike and I scurried down the stairs and she turned out the stair light after us. Mike saw me to my room and waited until I was tucked in bed.

"What about the shell?" I asked him.

He only shrugged. "What's the use of trying to figure Steven out?" he said. "Forget it. And next time don't let him get you up in the middle of the night."

When Mike had gone, leaving the light on beside my bed, I picked up the shell from where I'd left it on the quilt. It was a smooth, cool cone in my hand, and the brown splotches across creamy white seemed to shine in lamplight. But it told me nothing. I slipped it beneath my pillow and reached to turn off the light. Mike had closed my door, but I didn't bother to get up and open it. Somehow I knew that the room over-head would remain quiet for the rest of the night, and nothing would move around up there. Nevertheless, it was a long while before I fell asleep.

When I woke up the next morning it was twenty minutes to eight. I looked at my watch, remembering that somebody had said that breakfast was at eight.

But I lay still for a little while, trying to straighten out my thoughts and make some sort of plan for the day. I wanted to find out about that shell, for one thing. And today I would have to persuade Steven to help me with the play we would read for Alanna. That must be done before any more time slipped away. I thought about Gram too and wondered how she felt this morning. I knew Gramp would call us and let us know.

But in spite of all this thinking, I wasn't very sure of anything by the time I rolled out of bed and hurried through the bathroom and into my jeans and a sweater.

I knocked on Mike's door as I went past, because I knew he'd be oversleeping unless someone called him. When I went downstairs to the dining room I found everyone but Mike just sitting down at the table. Alanna looked pretty and slim in jeans and a cardigan, with her hair in a braid down her back, but she looked a little pale too. Cousin Daphne was gloomy. She hardly said good morning when I came into the room. Steven seemed to be interested mainly in food. Only Mr. Mercer was in a talkative mood.

"What was going on upstairs last night?" he said, when we'd all been served our scrambled eggs with bacon.

It developed that he had a small guest room on the main floor when he stayed at Burton Oliver's house, and that he had been sitting in the drawing room, where he'd poked up the fire and was reading a book. So he had heard us on the stairs.

"You'd better ask *her*," Cousin Daphne said with an edge to her voice as she nodded at me.

Alanna looked up quickly from her plate. "What is it? What happened?"

The room focused on me. Steven looked up from his food and seemed to be waiting for what I would say. I felt like telling *him* to explain what had happened, but I knew accusations would do no good. Again, I decided to say nothing about the shell. If Steven expected me to talk about it, I would fool him. I just repeated what we had told Cousin Daphne last night—that I'd heard a noise in the studio, and Mike and I had gone up there to see what had happened. And we had found a window open and had closed it. We had made enough noise so that Mrs. Price had wakened and had come to look in on us.

Steven said, "You went into the studio in the middle of the night?" and there was almost a note of admiration in his voice.

I felt like reminding him that he had gone there first to let down that spool of thread with the shell tied to the end of it. Because if it hadn't been Steven, who could it possibly have been? Not Alanna. Not Cousin Daphne. Not Harry Mercer. Not even old Mr. Burton Oliver.

Mike came in just then and saved me from answering. As we finished breakfast, Alanna suggested that we all go skiing that morning, and that is what was arranged. Before we left, Gramp called to say that Gram had had a good night.

Mr. Mercer stayed home, but the rest of us, including Cousin Daphne, went out on the slopes and had a lovely time all morning. Alanna wouldn't let us go down Devil's Drop, but we skied the next best slope and everything was fine. Steven cheered up and was almost friendly while we were on skis. He loved to ski and he couldn't be gloomy when he was out on the slopes doing something he managed so well.

Afterward, drinking hot chocolate in the restaurant, we were like any friendly, happy family, and gloom didn't descend on us again until we were on the way home. It was as if the old house, and the very prospect of returning to it, depressed us all. Alanna grew uneasy again, as if she was fearful about something. And Steven put on his usual unfriendly scowl. Cousin Daphne turned from a bright orange bird into a black crow again, and the house took over our mood.

Before that, one special thing happened on the way home. Mike said he thought we ought to stop at Gramp's to see how Joe Reed was doing, and Alanna agreed that it would be a good idea. We went up the drive and parked beside the house. Everything looked deserted. The house was locked and still, and Joe was nowhere in sight. Mike and I got out of the car to look for him, and we went into his living quarters beside the garage. The place was empty, though a fire was burning in the wood stove.

"Maybe he's gone on a picnic to the cabin," I suggested to Mike.

Mike thought that was silly. "If he went to the cabin, it would be to get off by himself, and there's no one here to get away from."

I found a piece of paper and wrote Joe a note saying that we had looked in and that Gramp had phoned to say Gram was better and would have some tests today.

Then we headed back to the car. Just as we went down the drive and out to the road, I looked back and saw Joe standing near the garage looking after us. But it didn't seem worthwhile to tell Alanna to turn around and go back. So I let it go. I've wondered since if it would have made any difference in all that happened afterward if I had asked her to stop the car right then.

—11
Steven's Mural

After lunch Mr. Mercer went out, Alanna lay down for a nap, and Cousin Daphne went upstairs to tend Mr. Oliver. Mike asked permission to practice on his guitar and closed himself in the drawing room, where he wouldn't bother anyone. That gave me my chance with Steven, so I followed him around whether he liked it or not.

He had decided to work on his mural, and I asked if I could watch. When he gave his permission, grudgingly, I found a stool I could carry into the mural room, since it was unfurnished. The mural was to be a surprise for Alanna, so Steven chose times to work on it when she wouldn't interrupt him.

I sat down on my stool while he folded back the screens that hid the painting, and I watched while he went to work. I was wondering how to bring up the subject of the play without annoying him all over again. There didn't seem to be any way, and my thoughts turned again to last night.

Steven was working on the *Lilac Grove* section with his tempera paints and as he worked he began to talk, unexpectedly, about his father.

"Dad's a pretty good artist. I guess that's why I like to paint. Before he got—sick—he did some really good work. I wish I could see my father."

"Won't your mother let you?" I asked.

128

"She thinks he's bad for me. She has a court order against him, unless he changes."

"How do you mean—'changes'?"

"Oh, I don't want to talk about it!" Steven cried, although it was he who had brought up the subject.

I felt sorrier than ever for him because I knew how dreadful it would be if I couldn't see my father.

We were quiet for a while, but I could feel a question coming up inside me—a question that sooner or later had to be asked.

"Why did you tap on my window last night?" I asked.

Steven went right on with his painting, concentrating as if he hadn't heard me.

"With the shell," I added. "Why did you tap on my window with that shell?"

This time he heard me and turned to stare. "What are you talking about? Why should I tap on your window? And how, when it's two stories up?"

I answered him patiently. "You tied a shell to a spool of thread and let it down outside my window from the monster room. In the middle of the night. You wanted to wake me up. Why?"

He looked at me as if I'd taken leave of my senses and then went back to his painting. "I don't know what you're talking about. And I never got out of bed last night at all."

"You don't have to lie about it," I said. "Who else would do a thing like that?"

"Maybe someone who wanted to get me into trouble." He spoke over his shoulder without turning around, so I couldn't see his face.

I hadn't thought of that. I hadn't thought that perhaps some grown-up might want to make me think Steven was playing tricks. And make others think that too? I could imagine Cousin Daphne doing something mean like that. But I still wasn't sure about Steven.

"Anyway, I can't see that it makes any sense," I said. "Why should anyone want to wake me like that and try to frighten me?"

"If you were scared, why did you go upstairs to what you call the 'monster room'?"

"I didn't intend to. I got Mike up and told him what happened, and he started upstairs right away. So I followed him. But there was no one there—just an open window and a spool of thread."

Steven added a bit of blue paint to the figure that represented a dancing Alanna and said nothing for a moment or two. Then he spoke over his shoulder again.

"How do you know it was a shell tapping on your window?"

"I opened the window and reached out and took hold of it. The thread snapped, and I was left with the shell."

"Have you still got it?"

"Of course. Do you want to see it?"

"Sure," Steven said. "Get it and bring it here."

I went out into the hall and was in time to surprise Cousin Daphne and Harry Mercer whispering together. They looked as though they might be arguing about something. When she saw me Cousin Daphne frowned and began to talk nervously.

"Grandfather is always complaining. I never have a moment's peace."

Mr. Mercer said, "Well, what do you expect when he's old and ill?"

As I went on to my room, I had a feeling that it wasn't old Mr. Oliver they had been talking about before I appeared.

Before I'd gone downstairs for breakfast I had taken the shell from under the pillow and put it in my suitcase. I opened the case and rummaged around till I found the shell in a pocket. Once more I turned it around in my hands, seeking for some answer, but it had nothing to say to me. As I carried it back to Steven along the hall, I could hear the faraway strumming of Mike's guitar. He was still busy with his practicing. Cousin Daphne and Mr. Mercer were gone.

Steven took the shell in one hand without putting down his paintbrush, and whistled softly. "This is from a shell collection of mine. I took some shells upstairs to Grandfather Burton's room to amuse him, and this is one of them. Anyone could get it from his room and use it as you say they did."

"But why?"

Steven gave the shell back to me. "Who knows with something as crazy as this? To scare you, maybe? To make you afraid to stay here in this house?"

I couldn't see that I would be a threat to anyone in the house, so that didn't make any sense. I sat down on the stool again and put the shell on the floor beside me. For a while I was quiet, and Steven concentrated on his painting. But my mind wasn't quiet. This was my one chance to be alone with Steven. I had to get up the courage to ask him that next question. The one that was so important to me. But I sat still for a while and let him paint.

"I asked you once before," I said finally, "but I have to ask you again. I want terribly to read something for Alanna so she can judge whether I have any acting talent. She said I should get you to help me. She said you read very well and you could help me with a part from one of the plays you've written."

Steven made a snorting sound but said nothing.

"It's such a little thing to do," I said. "But it means such a lot for me."

"Why should I?" Steven said.

"Don't you ever feel that you'd like to do something kind for someone?" I asked.

Steven flushed darkly and was silent. I knew my words must have stung him, but he really deserved it.

"It's just that you seem to have set yourself against me right from the beginning," I said. "And I don't know why."

He said something surprising then, almost blurting it out. "I don't know why either."

Perhaps I could see how that might be. He was a mixed-up sort of boy who felt his mother didn't appreciate him, and as a result he resented everyone. Perhaps especially someone who thought his mother was wonderful and sought her out. But he had more going for him than he seemed to understand. I offered him my own thoughts a little uncertainly.

"Alanna is going to love that mural when you show it to her. I know she'll be pleased and proud."

He snorted again. "That's how much you know! She's going to hate it and hate me. And that's fine!"

He had tried to tell me that before, but I still didn't understand.

"I don't see why."

He waved a hand at the empty sections of the painting that represented the beginning of Alanna's career. "Wait till she sees what I do with those! She'll be furious. Her feelings will be hurt plenty and she'll probably hate me."

The way he spoke shocked me. For a moment I couldn't say anything. At last I found the words I had to speak.

"In that case, Steven, why do you have to paint those squares? Why don't you just leave them out? Why do you have to hurt her and make her angry?"

"Because she deserves it," he said in a low, deadly voice.

I felt a little sick. It seemed a terrible thing that he should want to hurt his mother, when she obviously loved him very much and worried about him.

"I think you're wrong about her," I said softly.

He began to clean a brush, working with quick, angry gestures. "You don't know anything about it. You've only just met her. You don't know what she's like. What a fake she is."

"I think she's like her movies, really. No matter what may have happened back in the beginning, she's like her movies now."

Steven turned his back on me and said nothing, and I puzzled over him in silence. Quite clearly, he had poured a lot of time and painstaking effort into the work he had done on this mural. Whether he believed it or not, he had poured love into it. Yet in some twisted way he felt that he had to do something terrible with those early squares—something that would hurt and anger his mother. I wished with all my heart that I could find a way to make him see the truth. Because if he took a happier course, he would be a happier boy. But I hadn't any idea how to help him. I only wished that I could.

"Anyway," I said, "none of this has anything to do with your helping me to read a few scenes from a play for your mother. I still don't see why you can't help me with that. There isn't any reason why you should be angry with me, is there?"

"Maybe there is," he said. "You come around where you're not wanted. Not even Cousin Daphne wants you in the house. I can tell from things she said. You make extra work and bother, but Mother doesn't consider anyone else."

"She'll help me if you'll do this one little thing that I've asked. So why can't you?"

He turned his head to give me a long stare, but before he could say anything more, a tapping sounded on the door, and Alanna's voice called out.

"Steven, are you there?"

He went past me and opened the door a crack. "You can't come in here now."

"Why not? Steven, I—"

"I'm making something," he said, "and it's a secret. Jan is here watching me, but she won't tell you either. So just go away."

I could see her in the crack past Steven, and I saw her face light up. "Are you making something for me, Steven?"

"Maybe," he said.

She looked so pleased and happy that I almost wanted to cry. Because in the end she was going to be hurt if Steven kept on the course he chose to follow.

"All right," she said almost gaily. "Then I won't come in. I only wanted to ask if you're going to help Jan read a part from one of your plays."

I was sorry she had brought that up herself. I still thought I might find a way to persuade him, and she had said she would leave it up to me. But if he refused her too, he'd think he'd have to stick by it.

"I don't know," he said. "Maybe I will."

"Fine," Alanna said through the crack in the door. "Why don't you do that last fantasy you wrote—the one about the girl who is adopted by a witch? But I won't push you. I know you'll pick the one you think best."

She went off down the hall, whistling softly to herself, as though the encounter with Steven had cheered her up immensely. When she had gone I looked at Steven and waited.

He went back to cleaning brushes. "Do you want to look at that part now?" he asked.

I kept myself from sounding excited. "If it's all right with you," I said.

When he had finished with his cleanup, he picked up the binoculars from the window ledge and fixed them to his eyes. He was looking out toward the cabin again, and his face had darkened, as though he might start scowling any minute because of something he was thinking.

"Is anyone there?" I asked.

He shook his head and set the glasses down. Finally he said, "Come along," and started down the hall ahead of me. I picked up the shell from the floor and took it with me as he led the way back to his sitting room and began to rummage in his desk. In a moment he brought out a large black notebook and ran through several pages of pencil writing.

"I wish I could write," I said wistfully. "Your mother has so many things to be proud of you for. The way you can paint, and ski, and write. While I can't do anything well. I wish—"

"You can be yourself," Steven said surprisingly. "Everybody likes you easily. And nobody much likes me."

I could have told him that he didn't act very likable, but I decided not to. I didn't think that what Steven needed right now was unkindness.

"I like you," I said. "At least I do part of the time."

He threw me a quick look but didn't answer that. "You'd better read the play first, and then I'll tell you which scene I think you should do."

I set the shell down on his desk and took the black notebook, opened at the place where the play began. Steven wrote a strong, clear script that was easy to read, and I found myself very quickly caught up in the spell of the story.

Steven's witch was not the witch of most fairy stories. She was beautiful and blond and tall, and her name was Emeralda. She had a lovely singing voice and she went out sometimes to entertain the people. But she was truly a witch and she could cast spells and turn people into toads if they put themselves in her power.

One day a young girl named Sapphire came to her door—an orphan who was without a home and lost in the woods where the witch lived. Sapphire was taken in by Emeralda and promised a good home if she would do everything the witch said and give her all of her inner heart. The witch promised to make her beautiful and rich and enable her to marry a king's son.

The girl, however, kept a little piece of her inner heart for herself and in that little piece she didn't believe anything the witch said. And when the king's son, Prince Topaz, came to the door seeking her, she gave him that hidden piece of her heart that did not belong to the witch. When Emeralda discovered this she was furiously angry. She caused the girl to be dressed in rags and to lose all her outer beauty, so that she was just the plain little thing she had been when she came to the door. But the prince did not mind. Because he had that bit of her inner heart, he could sense Sapphire's beauty of spirit and he thought her face was beautiful since it reflected that spirit. He took her away in her rags to present her to his father the king, and her real beauty shone before the king and he accepted her as the one perfect wife for his son.

Once, when I had nearly finished reading, I heard the phone ring out in the hall and Alanna's voice answer it. But I was lost in the story and I didn't pay much attention.

"It's a lovely play," I said warmly when I had finished reading. "Look—it has made me cry."

Steven seemed to thaw a little toward me, to soften and become more gentle. But it wasn't in character for him to let me know that I'd pleased him.

"O.K.," he said. "Then you can take the book away and copy out all of your part—what Sapphire says. Put in all the cues too. They are the last words spoken each time before Sapphire speaks."

I blinked the wetness from my lashes and picked up the book. Other thoughts were coming to me now. Thoughts I didn't dare speak out to Steven. How much of the time had he been thinking of his mother when he wrote about the witch? There were little touches—sometimes loving, sometimes unkind—that made me think he had been making up his play about her.

"Take a scratch pad and pencil," Steven said, not guessing my thoughts. "When you've got the scene copied where the girl comes to the witch's house, you can come back and we'll read it together."

I stacked a scratch pad on top of the book and took a pencil from his desk. Then I picked up the shell.

"What do you want that for?" Steven said.

"I'll give it back to you after a while," I told him. "I just want to think about it some more. I still have a feeling that it was meant to tell me something, only I haven't figured out yet what it is." I had begun to believe Steven when he said he hadn't lowered it to my window.

Steven clearly thought that was nonsense, but since I'd liked his play, he was feeling more obliging, and he didn't object. Carrying my things, I left Steven in his room and went into the hall.

Alanna Graham stood beside the small table that held the telephone. The receiver was on the hook, but her hand was on it and she was staring as though it might come to life and bite her. Or had already bitten her. She looked so strange and lost that I was afraid to say anything to her. Even as I moved in her direction, she turned from the table and went toward the third-floor stairs, not seeing me.

I had to follow her. She was so many wonderful things to me, and now she was in some terrible trouble. She might need someone, want someone—if only to have me call Cousin Daphne or Harry Mercer. I had to follow and see if I could help. If she didn't speak to me, didn't see me, then it wouldn't matter.

She climbed the stairs slowly with one hand on the banister, moving like an old woman who had trouble putting one foot before the other. There was no one else around, and I didn't want to call Steven. This would be the wrong moment for him to be unsympathetic toward his mother. On the third floor she turned to the right, away from her grandfather's room, and when she came to the studio, she took down the key and unlocked the door. Then she went inside, leaving it open behind her.

This room, of all places, I didn't want to enter. But Alanna was in some terrible trouble and I wanted to go to her, to offer her whatever comfort I could. At least the room was filled with daylight, and all the stone figures stood motionless, their shadows thinner than they had been by moonlight. Alanna wove her way among them and went straight to the two windows that overlooked the garden and faced uphill toward Gramp's house. She chose one of them and stood with her forehead against the pane, looking down into the yard.

I stepped across the doorsill. "Alanna? Is something wrong? Is there anything I can do to help?"

She didn't look around, or even seem surprised. "Come in, young Jan. This is a good time for me to have someone with me. I am troubled, but I can't talk about it. Will you just be with me quietly for a few moments?"

"Of course," I said. I found the figures didn't frighten me so much with Alanna there as I went across the room to stand beside her at the window. I didn't say anything more, and for a moment she was silent too. Then she began to talk to me in a low, soft voice.

"Did you know, Jan, that my grandmother was killed in a fall from this window? I loved her very much. Sometimes we didn't understand each other when I was growing up, but I loved her. More than I did my grandfather. My parents were dead and she was like a mother to me. I must have disappointed her and hurt her very much when I was young. Often I wish she could be here now, because I know she'd have been proud of me. She wouldn't have wanted anything terrible to happen to me. As it may."

She broke off and looked at me for the first time, her eyes filled with tears.

"But I mustn't tell you all this, Jan. I mustn't worry you. It's just that you have a sympathetic heart and you wear it on your sleeve for anyone to see. I'm sure you must find that people like to talk to you, tell you things."

I supposed that was true, though I'd never thought much about it.

"You can tell me anything you like, Alanna," I said. "I know it helps to talk to someone sometimes. And if it's secret, I won't tell. You can trust me on that."

She caught her breath in something like a sob. "I'm sure I can, Jan dear. But I haven't grown so weak as all that. Not yet. It's just that I need to think. I need to make a terrible decision. That's why I came here to this room."

She meant because of the phone call, I knew. Someone was calling her who upset her badly.

"Sometimes in the past," she went on, "when I've stood at this window, I could imagine my grandmother near, listening to me, counseling me. Her death was so tragic. She had a fainting spell, a dizzy spell, when she was sitting in the open window one October day. The screen was out and she simply went over the sill to her death. It was unfortunate that it had to happen in this room, because that gave rise to superstitious talk."

"Talk?" I echoed softly.

"Yes. We had a foolish young girl working for us at that time and she was frightened of this room. She said one of Grandfather Burton's sculptured figures moved and pushed Grandmother out of the window. After that, the story crept all around the village, and by this time we have a firm reputation for living in a haunted house. Grandfather could never manage without Cousin Daphne because the maids never stay for long. But, of course, Cousin Daphne has very little that's her own and she has been given a home and a good income here all these years in return. So the bargain has been a good one, even though she rebels at times."

I was close enough beside her to look through the glass and down to the paved walk below, where Mrs. Oliver had fallen. The window glass was icy to my touch and I shivered there beside Alanna. The sound behind us was so faint, that for a moment I didn't turn. I felt eerily that one of the figures might have taken a step nearer to us. Then we turned together, Alanna and I, and were in time to see the door close gently, secretly, and to hear the sharp click of the twisting key.

Someone had locked us in the room.

—12
Locked In

It was frightening to hear the grate of that key in the lock and know that we couldn't get out of the room. I drew closer to Alanna. Strangely, she did not seem especially upset and she smiled at me, though a little ruefully.

"That's Steven's mischief again, of course. Don't worry about it. When it pleases him he'll let us out. And we'll fool him by not being disturbed or frightened."

I think my face must have shown that I was frightened, for Alanna patted my hand and went to the door. When she had tried it, she came back to me.

"It's locked, all right. That means we have time to ourselves. Until someone opens that door."

"Aren't you going to call?" I asked. "Aren't you going to make someone hear you?"

"Why should I? Daphne's out somewhere. Harry's downstairs and Steven's back in his room by now. Unless he's lingering in the hall to see if we squeal. Only we'll show him—we won't make a sound."

She took a few quick little steps among the sculptured figures, not touching any of them. Then she bowed to the girl with the baby dragon in her hand and smiled at me.

"Don't you see, Jan? It's like an ocean voyage or a train trip. No one can bother us. We have no responsibilities. For this little while we can do as we please."

I wasn't altogether reassured, and Alanna was aware of the frightened look I cast at the stone figures gathered around us.

"You mustn't worry about Grandfather's sculptures," she said. "He was only portraying his vision of life. There's something wonderfully mysterious about them, you know, something wonderfully imaginative."

"But why—monsters?" I asked.

"They're the troubles of the world that men have to face. Some men are afraid, and Grandfather has shown their fears. But others stand up to the terrors and win against them—and he's shown that too. There are troubles in the world that must be struggled against. So this is a brave room, a room of courage, which is why I like to come here."

I looked about me with new eyes and saw that not all the faces were frightened. Some of them were facing life with a clear courage that would help them defeat their monsters. For the first time I felt better about the room.

"Enough of that," Alanna said. She waved a hand toward the notebook and pad I still held. "That's the book of Steven's plays, isn't it? So why don't you read a part for me? This is a perfect time. Did he pick the play you were to use?"

"Yes. It's the one about the witch that you suggested. But I haven't had time to copy out the part, and—"

"That doesn't matter. I know the witch's role by heart. We put it on for fun last Christmas when we were here, and we got one of the girls from town to play Sapphire, though she wasn't very good. I was Emeralda, and Steven was Topaz. We had fun. I'm sure I still remember the words. Here—let me see."

She took the book from me and riffled through it to the right place. Her eyes scanned the pages for a few moments and then she handed it back to me.

"Yes. I remember. I'll begin with the 'Come in out of the storm, child,' speech, and we can go on from there."

So that was what we did. There in that strange room of hovering figures we read the scene from Steven's play in which Sapphire arrives at the witch's cottage. And I know it didn't go very well. I wasn't familiar with the words and I stumbled over them. What was worse, I couldn't get inside Sapphire because I was too deeply inside me. I was thinking about the big dark house all around us and about being locked in by a cruel Steven. And of this spooky room from which Burton Oliver's wife had fallen to her death. Nevertheless, I kept on. I read the words doggedly, and I did try—if not my best, at least I tried.

When we had run through the scene, Alanna smiled at me. "Fine," she said. "Now we'll go over it again. An actor has to get used to words and feel comfortable with them before he can really play a role."

So we went through it again, and even though I didn't stumble over the words as badly, it wasn't any good. I couldn't get the feeling right. Alanna continued to be undisturbed. She kept explaining to me that it took time for an actor to get caught up in a role. I must take the time to rehearse these words when I was alone. Then I'd get the feeling of them.

While we were attempting the scene for the third time, there was a sudden loud crash in the next room. That was the room where Alanna kept her movie things and it sounded as though someone had fallen down among them.

We stared at each other in dismay, and Alanna gave up her pretense of being off on an ocean voyage. She ran to the door of the studio and began to bang and call for someone to come and let us out. In a few moments we heard steps on the stairs as Cousin Daphne and Harry Mercer came running up. One of them turned the key in the lock and opened the door, and they stared in at us in amazement. Cousin Daphne still had her coat on and had apparently just got home.

Alanna paid them little attention. "Something fell in the next room!" she cried. "We must see what happened right away."

She rushed past them and opened the door of the movie room, and I ran right after her. I was there behind her when she went into the room. Here the lights had been turned on because the blinds were drawn. Someone lay on the floor, with the dress dummy toppled across him. We stepped closer and saw that it was the pajamaed figure of old Mr. Oliver.

Cousin Daphne cried out and ran to kneel beside him. "Grandfather Burton!" she cried. "What has happened to you?"

The old man didn't answer, and under Cousin Daphne's direction Harry Mercer picked him up and carried him back to his bed, where he lay against his pillows looking very white, with his eyes closed.

"He must have walked in there by himself!" Alanna said, shocked.

"I've suspected for some time that he could get around," Cousin Daphne said.

"Then you'd better give him a talking to." Mr. Mercer sounded irritable. "He shouldn't be stumbling around by himself."

"What did he want in that room?" Alanna said. "Why should he get out of bed and go wandering around in there?"

No one had the answer to that.

I had followed the others into Mr. Oliver's room and now I stood close to Alanna beside the bed. A strange thought had come to me. If the old man could move around, perhaps it was he who had locked us into the studio. So that he could do as he liked without interference? Perhaps it hadn't been Steven at all.

His eyelids fluttered and he opened his eyes. Strangely, I was the one his gaze rested on first. Perhaps because I was not so tall as the others, and I was close to the bed, standing there holding the notebook and pad and shell. His eyes seemed to focus and his look dropped to the things in my hands.

"Inside," he said faintly. "Look inside, little girl."

The others didn't understand his words, any more than I did, and Cousin Daphne bent to help him sit up. She gave him a capsule and some water to drink, and in a few moments he was a little stronger.

"So you can move around?" Alanna said to him, still amazed.

He grinned at her slyly. "I don't want to be helpless, the way you all want to make me. I manage to keep up my strength. I manage to get around."

"Well, you mustn't anymore," Cousin Daphne said. "You could have injured yourself badly when you fell."

"It was that dratted dress dummy. I caught a pajama button on the lace dress and pulled it over on top of me. Wouldn't have fallen otherwise."

"He must rest now," Cousin Daphne said.

The old man tried to rouse himself in the bed, and he reached a wavering hand in my direction. But before he could say anything more, Cousin Daphne had shooed us all out of the room.

"So it wasn't Steven," I said to Alanna when we were out in the hall. "It wasn't Steven who locked us in the room."

She nodded uncertain agreement. "It looks as though it might have been Grandfather. Though I don't understand what he could possibly have been after in that next room."

"He ought to be put into a nursing home," Mr. Mercer said as we started downstairs, but Alanna shook her head emphatically. "This is his home. And he has Daphne to take care of him. So I won't have him moved. He's best off here. And if he can get about, perhaps we should encourage that and not let him fool us anymore."

On the second floor I looked helplessly at Alanna, and she smiled at me. "Don't look so woebegone. I've told you that the best actor doesn't read a new part well in the beginning. Why don't you take that book to your room and study it for a while? Then we'll try again."

She was kind and encouraging, but I felt very discouraged. I knew how awful I had been. But I did as she said and carried my things to my own room. There was a silence from downstairs that meant Mike wasn't playing his guitar anymore, and I tiptoed past his room so he wouldn't come out and ask questions. In my own room I closed the door and carried notebook, pad, and shell over to the desk and set them down.

What had Mr. Oliver meant by that one word, "inside"? He hadn't referred to the scratch pad. And he couldn't have known about Steven's black notebook. I began to tingle with realization and a certain excitement. The shell—he had meant the shell!

And if he did—then it meant that it was he who had crept out of bed in the middle of the night and gone to the studio to let that shell down on its spool of thread to make it tap at my window. Why? Why all the secrecy? And why had he picked me?

Inside what? Inside the shell?

Once more I examined it, but there was nothing in view. I found a nail file in my suitcase and poked the end of it beneath the curved lip of the cone. Something seemed to stick, to crackle. There was something there. It took me quite a bit of poking to hook on to the folded bit of paper inside the shell and edge it out. The moment I could catch hold of a corner of it, I pulled it loose.

The paper was small because it had been folded over

several times. I opened it with fingers that shook a little from excitement. A few words had been scrawled on it in ink in a wavering hand.

"Come to see me *alone*. B.E.O."

"Alone" had been underlined. And the initials clearly stood for Burton E. Oliver. I read the five words several times, then folded the paper and thrust it into a pocket of my jeans. Why should he want to see me? I felt bewildered and a little shivery. I certainly didn't want to go into that room alone and talk to that old man.

Another thought came to me. If he was moving around secretly and up to all sorts of mischief, it was probably he who had shoved the figures around in the studio and made it seem as though they were moving about among themselves. He was a wicked old man, and I didn't want to go near him.

But I could go near Steven. There was no reason why I shouldn't show him the note to see if he knew what it meant, so I went down the hall to Steven's room.

He and Mike were playing Scrabble at the center game table. Steven looked up as I came in. "Have you copied out your part, Jan?"

I shook my head. "I haven't had time. You don't know all that's been happening. Your grandfather got out of his bed and locked your mother and me in his studio."

For once I had taken both boys by surprise. They stared at me and after a moment Steven spoke.

"You'd better tell the rest," he said. "Whatever are you talking about?"

I told them the whole story, winding up with the finding of the note. Steven began to chuckle before I was through, and he seemed to get quite a bang out of the fact that his great-grandfather had been tricking the whole house over his supposed inability to get about.

"Anyway, I can now come off the list of chief suspects," Steven said. "What do you suppose the old boy is up to? I'll have to watch and let you know when you can get into his room by yourself, Jan. Then you can find out what he wants."

"But I don't want to go in there," I said. "The very idea makes me feel creepy. I don't want to see him alone."

"Just the same, you'll have to," Steven said. "You can't put him to all that trouble over something he very much wants and then not carry through with it."

That was silly. *I* hadn't put him to any trouble, and I started to tell Steven so, when he jumped up from the game table.

"Now would be a good time. You said Cousin Daphne gave him a capsule. That's probably to make him relax and sleep. So she'll leave him by himself. But those things don't work as fast as all that. I'll take you up there and wait outside the door. Then you needn't be afraid of him. You can call me if anything happens. We've got to find out what he wants."

There was no resisting Steven. He and Mike came upstairs with me and I found myself being shoved into old Mr. Oliver's room.

The old man lay in the bed with his eyes closed. I found myself hoping he was already asleep, but the floor creaked as I came close and he opened his eyes and grinned at me.

"You found the note, didn't you?" he said. "So you came to see me alone. You're a good girl."

His voice was weak, but his eyes had a sparkle to them. Suddenly I stopped being afraid. He was only a sick old man who wanted something very much. And he had once been rather a great person who had made all those imaginative figures in the studio.

"Why did you want to see me?" I said.

"Because you may be able to help me. I can't ask any of the others. They mustn't know."

I thought of Steven and Mike outside the door, but Mr. Oliver's voice was so faint that I could scarcely hear it, and it wouldn't carry that far.

"How can I help you?" I said.

His wrinkled eyelids fluttered and finally opened wide so he could look at me. "Because I've lost something. I've tried to look for it myself, but I can't find it. And I'm not strong enough to go all over the house."

He stopped speaking, as though he was suddenly out of breath, and I cast an uneasy glance toward the door. It was open, but I couldn't see the boys. I was beginning to feel sorry for old Mr. Oliver and not so afraid of him.

"Why did you lock us in that room?" I said.

His mouth stretched in its sly grin. "Daphne had gone out and I wanted to have time to look without being interrupted. Were you scared?"

"Alanna wasn't scared. She almost liked it. Something's been worrying her—"

But he wasn't interested in that. "About this thing I want you to find for me—it's a strongbox made of gray steel, and it's locked. I've kept it for years right here in this room. Not so long ago it disappeared, and I haven't seen it since. The contents should never be looked at by anyone but me. It's very important and I don't know who has taken it or why."

A strongbox? Then I knew where it was! So this was Steven's doing. I was glad he couldn't hear the old man, because I had a feeling that Steven would not willingly give up the box.

"Maybe I can find it for you," I said softly.

"I don't know why I kept those things," he said, not hearing me. "No one should see them. And yet I left they had to be kept."

I bent toward him and put a hand lightly on his arm. "Mr. Oliver, I think I know where the box might be. I'll try to find it for you."

The capsule was beginning to take effect and he looked at me drowsily. "I knew you were a good girl. I like mischief. I like to tease people. It's all I have to do these days. But this has gone beyond teasing. This means hurt and trouble."

"I'll do what I can about the box," I whispered, close to his ear.

He went quietly to sleep and I left the room. The boys were waiting for me in the hall, and I knew by their faces they hadn't been able to hear.

"He's gone to sleep," I said.

"What did he want of you?" Steven demanded eagerly.

I shook my head at him. "I don't want to talk about it. He doesn't want anyone else to know."

Steven wasn't pleased, and even Mike was disgusted with me.

"He probably doesn't know what he's doing," Mike said. "You can't pay any attention to an old man like that."

But I knew I would pay attention to him. Mr. Oliver was truly worried about something, and if I could help him to get that box to a safe place, I would.

As soon as I could, I got away from Steven and Mike and went to tell Alanna that I was going outside for a while. She didn't mind, so I put on my outdoor things and started off as secretly as I could for the cabin.

It was a short walk from the big house to the end of the trail leading down from the slopes. The cabin was at the fork of the trail where the path began that led to the road and Gramp's house. No one seemed to be around, inside or out, though I looked through the windows before I opened the door.

When I stepped into the main room the emptiness seemed to press in around me, and I wished Mike were along, or Steven. But I knew I had to do this by myself. Even though a look through the windows told me the kitchen section of the cabin was empty, it took me a moment to get up my courage to open the door. I was right—the kitchen was empty, and very still.

It took me only a moment to carry the stool over where I could climb onto it and reach the cupboard door. I pulled it open, afraid that the box would be gone. But it was still there, its cold gray steel dull in the late afternoon light. I reached for it with both hands and lifted it down from the shelf. It wasn't very heavy.

As I set the box on the kitchen table, I noticed for the first time that the key was in the lock. It had not been there the last time I'd seen the box. I wondered if Steven had been here and had forgotten to take away the key. Or perhaps he thought it wouldn't matter. That no one would come here to look into it. I pulled off my mittens. As if drawn by a magnet, my fingers moved to the key. The box was locked, but I had only to turn that key and the lid would open.

The cabin seemed unbearably still. The key was cold metal in my fingers. Slowly I turned it in the lock.

—13

Face at the Window

When the box was unlocked, I raised the lid. A few papers and clippings lay folded in the bottom—not a great deal of contents to be locked away. But I recognized the top item. It was the same gray photographic folder that I had found when I had broken Alanna's Greek jar. I picked it up and opened it to look at it again.

Yes—the picture was of Alanna when she was very young, and she looked unhappy and frightened. Someone had bothered to put this newsprint picture in a folder, probably to preserve it. But now I found that I could take it out easily and there was printing which had been hidden by the rim of the folder. I read the words under the picture.

Anna Oliver coming from her trial after being sentenced to prison.

So that was the secret in Alanna Graham's past! I knew that if I took out the other papers and clippings, the whole story would be revealed. But somehow I didn't want to know it in this ugly way. There was a real story here, but Alanna herself ought to be the one to tell it—if she chose. I put the picture back in the folder and the folder in the box. Then I climbed onto the stool again and restored the steel box to its cupboard shelf and closed the door. I didn't want to take this box back to Mr. Oliver. I had a feeling that Steven had had the right idea when he had brought it out here. No one would look into it here, as they might at the house. Since Steven had already looked through the contents they could no longer be hidden from him. Perhaps I would tell him what I knew and ask him what I'd better do about Mr. Oliver's request. Things had changed now that I knew what was in the box.

I pushed the stool away from the cupboard and went out of the cabin. And I hurried all the way back to the house. I felt a little sick over my discovery. How terrible for Alanna that she had this secret in her past—something she had long ago lived down but hadn't wanted her son to know. Tears burned my eyes at the thought of her suffering over old mistakes. I wasn't curious. I didn't want to know what had happened to her unless she told me.

Steven and Mike were still playing Scrabble up in Steven's room when I got there. I took off my parka and went in to speak to them. I didn't mind about Mike knowing. He was my brother.

"Your great-grandfather is worried about his lock-box," I said to Steven. "He wanted me to find it and bring it back to him. But it's still in the cabin."

Steven fumbled among the Scrabble pieces, taken by surprise. "What do you know about that box?"

"Mike and I found it in the cabin when we were there. And I told Mr. Oliver I'd try to get it for him. This time you left the key in the lock."

I don't know what tiny sound made me turn and look at the doorway just then, but I was in time to see Cousin Daphne standing there looking in. I didn't know how much she might have heard, but when she saw she'd been noticed she went quickly away.

If Steven saw her, he paid no attention, and his scowl was back. "So I suppose you had to snoop? I suppose you opened the box?"

"I needed to open it," I said. "I needed to know what I was doing."

"So now you know the truth about my mother? So now you know what a fake she is. All that stuff about her being good and honest and open about everything! And none of it is true."

"Say," Mike put in, "what's all this about anyway?"

With a quick motion of his hands Steven mixed up the Scrabble game, scattering the pieces.

"Wait," I said. "You don't have to say anything more. I looked at that picture that was on top of everything else. But I didn't dig into the other things. I don't really know what happened, so you don't have to tell us."

"I might as well," Steven said darkly. "After she ran away from home my mother started running with a crowd that was no good. She was in love with a boy who was mixed up in armed robbery. The gang was caught, and my mother was one of them. She was sentenced to prison and served most of her term before she was let out on parole. It's all there in those papers my great-grandfather kept. She never told me anything about it. And her public doesn't know. Audiences everywhere think she's a lovely, honest person, and—"

"But she is," I said to Steven. "Of course she is. Because she has made up for what happened in the past. You can't be so cruel as to hold those things against her."

"Why didn't she tell me the truth, if she's so honest?" he cried. "I found that box in Great-grandfather Burton's room, and I knew where he kept the key. So one time when he was asleep, I went through it and I read everything. I meant to show my mother that picture in the folder, but I couldn't. No matter what awful things she'd done, I couldn't face her with them. Then the picture disappeared. Maybe Great-grandfather took it out of the box. Anyway, the more I thought of that box being there in the open in Great-grandfather's room, where Cousin Daphne or anybody could look into it, the more I couldn't stand it. It was safer to take it away and hide it in the cabin. Only now it's not even safe there, with you kids going in and out, and that man, whoever he is, using it for some purpose."

"We know who the man is," Mike said. "It's only Joe Reed, our grandfather's handyman. He likes to picnic in the cabin, and he's stocked it with some food and things. But I don't think he'd look into that box."

"He might steal the box," Steven said sharply. "He might even use it for blackmail if he got hold of it. Maybe he already has. What about those phone calls my mother gets that upset her so much? After I found out about the box, I wondered if someone was trying to blackmail her because of the past. Trying to threaten her with exposure if she didn't pay him money. If all this ever came out about her, all her audiences that trust her and think she's so wonderful would turn against her."

"How awful!" I said.

"You can't think Joe Reed—" Mike began, but Steven broke in right away.

"Why can't I? Someone's after her about something. He could have found that box."

"Then it would be your fault," I said. "Though I don't really think Joe Reed would—"

Steven made a really horrible face and scowled more fiercely than ever. "I don't care if it is my fault. I don't care what happens to her now that I know what she's like."

I didn't believe that. He kept contradicting himself— trying to protect the box, and then saying he didn't care what happened. Steven was as mixed up a boy as I'd ever seen and I would have given anything to help straighten him out and get him to think more kindly about his mother. I knew there wasn't any use arguing with him, but I had to try.

"That isn't really true," I told him. "You love her a lot. If you'd just go and talk to her about all this, you could clear everything up between you."

"Love her!" He echoed my words in a hard, angry voice.

"Yes. You've proved it by all the work you put into that mural. And by the way you took the box out of the house so no one would find it and look at what was inside. You——"

"That's right," he said. "The mural! I'll go and finish it now. I'll paint in those prison scenes I've planned for the beginning. When I give it to her she'll know I know the truth about her, and that I'll never believe in her again."

He began to gather up his painting things, but before he could collect them and rush off to the small room where his pictures were spread behind their screens, Alanna came into the room.

Steven had his back to her, so she didn't notice his face. "I have a plan," she said. "After dinner, let's read Steven's play clear through. That will give Jan a chance to get familiar with the way the whole thing sounds out loud. I can remember my part, and I'm sure you remember the part of Prince Topaz, Steven. It will be a good time to try it out."

Steven turned around then and she saw his face. Her fingers flew to her lips and she stared at him in dismay.

"Steven—whatever's the matter?"

"I don't want to read that old play," he said, his face flushed and his eyes all too bright with anger.

She didn't know why he was angry, and I could see the hurt come into her face. The last thing I wanted by this time was any more reading of that play, which would show up how terrible I was. But something had to be done, for Alanna's sake.

"Please, Steven," I said. "It would be a wonderful chance for me. The whole play deserves to be read—not just one scene picked out of the rest. Perhaps I can do better if I get the feeling of the entire play."

For some strange reason his expression softened as he looked at me. Perhaps he remembered in spite of himself how I had defended his mother. I pressed my advantage at once.

"Please, Steven. It's such a little thing for you to do. And even if I'm not any good, I'd love to see how you and your mother do the rest of the scenes."

Perhaps he didn't really want to paint those prison scenes into the mural. He had been postponing them all this time. He knew that once they were painted the mural would be spoiled for giving his mother any pleasure. So perhaps he was willing to postpone that time a little longer. I don't think he really knew what he wanted, but he was apt to rush in wildly and do something reckless unless he was stopped.

Unexpectedly he began to put his painting things away. He gave a little shrug of his shoulders, and though his face stayed dark and brooding, I knew we had won him over—for a little while longer, at least.

Mike had to be told what this was all about, and I did that as the others got ready for dinner. After we ate, the four of us went to the drawing room. In the hall Thor got up from sleeping near the foot of the stairs and came with us into the big room. Alanna flew about switching on lights, lighting the fire. When a portion of the room was bright, she waved us all into chairs. She was coaxing Steven now, trying to charm and win him, but he was still holding her off. He was in the right mood, anyway, to play the prince against the witch. Thor flopped on the floor before the fire and went back to sleep.

Mike started out to be our single audience, but
Cousin Daphne and Mr. Mercer heard us in the drawing room, and they came in to see what was happening.
Alanna captured them gaily as part of her audience.
She was a little too gay. I wondered if she was trying
to distract her own unhappy thoughts from whatever
was disturbing her. As she set the scene, explaining to
the audience about the witch's cottage in the woods, I
found myself thinking about what Steven had said.
About blackmail. About extorting money with a threat
of exposure.

Of course it needn't have anything to do with Joe
Reed or the contents of that box. Anyone at all could
have discovered the unhappy story of Alanna's past and
might be trying to get money out of her for the sake of
silence. If that was true, how frightened she must be!
I remembered how she had said that acting and her
present life were the things she most wanted. Yet if
what Steven suspected was true, and all the facts of her
trial and imprisonment were spilled out into the papers,
all that would be gone for her. Perhaps people were
more lenient about many things these days, and such
truths wouldn't bother a lot of actors. But Alanna
Graham was special. She was one of the last of the
really big stars, yet she was still young and adored and
highly thought of. Whole families went to see her pictures. There had never been any hint of scandal about
her. She held a position all by herself that could be
destroyed in an instant.

Alanna had brought Steven's black notebook from
my room and she handed it to me brightly. "Here you
are, Jan dear. Steven and I will play our roles from
memory, but you can read the part of Sapphire from
the notebook. Go ahead and find your place at the
beginning of the play."

I stole a quick look at Steven and found that he was
watching his mother in a glowering way. How hurt he

was, I thought. He so wanted her to be perfect, and he couldn't bear to find out that she hadn't always been what she pretended.

The play was in two acts, and we began reading with the first scene when Sapphire comes out of the woods, finds the cottage, and is welcomed inside by Emeralda.

Strangely, I think I did not read as badly as I had before, though I was no less distracted. I wasn't getting inside Sapphire or really getting caught up in the play, but it no longer seemed so desperately important to be good—so I was better. We read steadily through to the scene where the prince comes onstage and wants to take the maiden away. But the witch won't allow this. There is a good rousing scene between the witch and the prince, where the two are in conflict with each other, and Sapphire hovers around distracted and worried and a little frightened. I found I could do that part well, because that's the way I was feeling. Alanna stopped being the witch long enough to nod approvingly at me, and it occurred to me what a remarkable thing it was that *I* should be playing a scene with Alanna Graham.

When we finished the act, I found that it hadn't been so bad after all, and I was even beginning to feel a small sense of success. I was aware of Mike looking at me in surprise as the members of the audience clapped. We stirred around during the interval, since Alanna thought we should take a break. I got up to stretch my legs and went toward a window that overlooked a porch.

As I moved near the window something seemed to stir outside, and I caught a glimpse of a face pressed against the glass, dim in the lamplight. Startled, I realized that someone was out there, looking in. I stepped closer to see who it was, and the face faded away before my eyes. But not before I had recognized it. The man who had pressed his face against the window glass in order to look into the room was Joe Reed.

I acted fast then. I didn't explain what I meant to do or ask permission. I simply ran out of the room and outdoors, snatching up somebody's jacket from the rack near the door. Because I was so quick, I caught him on the driveway as he started off.

"Joe!" I called. "Wait a minute!"

I could see by the way he turned that he didn't want to wait, but since I had recognized him, he had to.

"Why were you looking in the window?" I cried as I caught up with him.

His eyes didn't meet mine. "I wanted to see if you and Mike were all right."

"Then why didn't you come to the door? Why did you sneak about looking in windows?"

"What difference does it make?" he said, sounding surly. "I didn't want to bother anybody." He changed the subject quickly. "How is your grandmother?"

"She's having tests. Gramp thinks they'll be home soon. She's feeling better."

"Good. I'll go along now."

He didn't bother to say good night but loped off along the drive. I was getting chilly, so I didn't look after him for long but hurried back inside the house. In the hallway I stood looking through the panes in the front door, trying to make out Joe Reed's vanishing figure. I didn't believe what he had told me—that he had wanted to know how we were. I remembered the time when I had seen him out on Gramp's terrace looking down toward the Oliver house. I remembered the night Thor had barked. The dog was asleep before the fire now and hadn't wakened. I remembered the time when Harry Mercer had come up to the house and to Joe's quarters out by the garage. Joe hadn't wanted to meet Mr. Mercer then but had slipped out of the room. And he had kept out of view when Alanna had driven us up to Gramp's to see him. Everything pointed to someone who had a very guilty conscience and was trying to keep out of sight. A blackmailer, perhaps?

"Jan? Where are you?" That was Alanna's voice.

I went back to the drawing room and took my place with the black notebook in my lap again. No one asked me where I'd been, and we went on with the next act. But I felt restless and uneasy now, and I found it hard to concentrate. Alanna looked at me in surprise once or twice, but I couldn't get hold of myself. The play had all slipped away from me. I couldn't have been more wooden and awkward in my part.

When we finished, Steven threw me a look of scorn. "Whatever made you think you could be an actress?" he said.

"Now, Steven." His mother tried to be soothing, but I knew she was disappointed.

"It doesn't matter," I said. "I don't think I really want to be an actress anyway."

"Well, horray!" Mike cried. "It's good you've come to your senses, because it sure doesn't look as though you ever could be one. It's a good play, though. And Steven and Alanna were fine. But why the prince would look at you more than once, I couldn't see. Mom and Dad will be relieved."

"She's all right as herself," Steven said, looking at me more kindly. "She just shouldn't get notions about being an actress."

Strangely, none of this hurt very much and I wondered in surprise if everyone had been right after all, and that this was just something I was naturally outgrowing. Though it left me with a feeling that I was back where I had started—with no talent of any kind, and no way to be anybody. The thing that troubled me most now was the empty feeling of not having any special purpose in my life.

At least working on the play seemed to have brought

us all together more amiably for a little while. Alanna began to plan skiing for the following morning, and that gave us something to look forward to. Steven was very quiet and I knew he was thinking his own dark thoughts, but at least he didn't behave any worse than usual, and he stayed away from working on the mural.

Nothing happened during the night, and I was glad of that. I didn't feel quite so concerned about the monster room upstairs, but just the same I left the door to the hall open when I went to sleep. I had considered going upstairs to see old Mr. Oliver to tell him where his box was, but there was no chance. After we were through with the play there was always someone with him, or else I was in a place where I couldn't sneak off by myself.

Anyway, I slept well that night and woke up in the morning feeling eager to go skiing. Everything was always better when we were out on the slopes. That's what I thought.

—14

Chase on the Mountain

The mountain was a pattern of black and white be-
neath a gray-white sky. It felt like snow, and white
clouds brought the smell of snow to the air. It was a
good day for skiing. Unfortunately Mike had caught a
cold, and Alanna didn't want him out on the slopes, so
he'd had to stay home. I said good-by to him regret-
fully, but he winked at me, and I had an uneasy feeling
that he might have some plan of his own in mind.

All the rest of the household had come out, even
Cousin Daphne and Mr. Mercer, and we were all going
up and down the slopes as fast as we could get places
on the chair lift. We weren't a happy group that morning, though. Cousin Daphne's orange parka didn't seem
to cheer her up, and she was behaving in a manner as
moody as Steven's. Mr. Mercer seemed to be watching
her in a secret sort of way. That is, he would stare at
her when he thought nobody was noticing and then
look quickly away if someone caught him with his eyes
on her. I had the curious feeling that something under-
ground was surfacing and that some sort of trouble lay
ahead. Alanna was trying to be brave and gay, but she
was uneasy too.

I was trying especially to keep an eye on Steven, because I wanted to find out if he had changed his mind
about the mural and if he felt a little better about his
mother now that he had spilled everything out to me.

Once, up at the top of the runs, he disappeared for a little while. I hadn't seen him go down, and I knew he had come up in the chair lift, so I started looking for him. We were all at the top at that time, but I poled myself away from the others and went beyond the top of the lift until I saw him. He was near the place where the trail started downhill over the back of the mountain toward the cabin that was located at its foot. Not a proper ski trail—just the path over the mountain. He was standing there with his back to me and he was talking to Joe Reed.

I began to push myself along faster because I certainly wanted to know what that was all about. Steven looked terribly excited about something, and even Joe looked different—not so glum and secretive as he usually looked. I had a sinking feeling as I saw them together because I was terribly afraid that Steven was once more engaged in betraying his mother. Or perhaps he didn't realize that Joe might be mixed up in blackmail and was the one who could be hurting his mother.

When I got near them Steven looked around and saw me. At once he was angry.

"Go away!" he shouted. "We don't want you here. Go away!"

Joe seemed uncomfortable. He didn't look at me but just stared off over the mountain as if he hadn't seen me and didn't know whom Steven was shouting at. There was nothing to do but turn around and go back to the others.

We had gone down the slopes and come up again before we found that this time Steven had really disappeared. We looked for him everywhere and Alanna began to get worried. I told her about seeing him with Joe Reed, Gramp's handyman, but that didn't mean anything to her, and I couldn't bring up the blackmail thing. I didn't know for sure. Though I began to wonder if Steven had been kidnapped by the blackmailer.

I was the one who saw Cousin Daphne slip away from the others at the top of the slope and start down the path that led to the cabin. She hadn't said anything to anyone about leaving us, and I began to feel uneasy about her as well. It had occurred to me that Joe and Steven might have gone down toward the cabin, and now Daphne was heading in that direction. Perhaps I'd better go too, I thought. That box might need protecting. I remembered the time I'd seen Daphne in the door of Steven's room when we'd been talking about where Mr. Oliver's steel box had been placed. She could very well have heard and be off to investigate it herself. And the key was waiting in the lock.

But when I would have started after her, something unpleasant happened. Mr. Mercer schussed over and put a hand on my shoulder.

"Come and ski down Hemlock with me," he said.

I tried to edge away from him, but he held on all the tighter.

"I don't want to," I said. "I think I'll ski down the trail to the cabin."

"No, you won't," he told me. "You're coming with me."

I had never liked Harry Mercer and now he was staring at me almost fiercely, as though he threatened me in some way. I looked around for Alanna, but I couldn't see her, and I knew I had to get away from Mr. Mercer. It was clear that he was determined to keep me from following Cousin Daphne. Everything seemed different and a little frightening. I had a feeling that something was up—something menacing that I didn't understand.

I gave a sudden quick wriggle that freed me from Mr. Mercer's hand, and a moment later I was skiing off toward the trail that led to the cabin. I knew I had to go that way. I had to follow Daphne. Mr. Mercer came after me at once, but I had the advantage of taking him by surprise, and I was already on the downhill trail and going fast.

Too fast. I realized quickly that this wasn't like skiing the slopes. The trail of snow ran between thick-growing trees and there was no width in which to christy back and forth and slow myself. If I tried to turn across the trail, I would slam into a tree or tangle my skis in undergrowth. Yet if I used the snowplow, I would go too slowly and Mr. Mercer would catch me.

I whooshed along, and though the slope was gentle, it headed straight downward and I was picking up speed. Finally there was only one thing to do, whether Mr. Mercer caught me or not. I sat down in the snow and slid to a halt. As I struggled to my feet, awkwardly because of my skis, I looked up the trail behind me and saw Mr. Mercer coming down fast.

Then, even as I watched, one of his skis struck a root in the path, the tip caught, and he flew into the air and came down with his skis releasing. I turned and started down the trail again. This time I went as fast as I dared, and then made sitzmarks again to slow myself. Mr. Mercer was nowhere in sight.

It seemed to take forever to get down the trail to the cabin. No one was in sight, but a pair of skis rested outside the door. Cousin Daphne's skis? I took my own off and put them beside hers. Just as I was about to go into the cabin, Mike came around a corner outside.

"Ssh!" he said. "She's in there with that box."

"You've got a cold and you're not supposed—" I began, but he hushed me again.

"I'm all right. It was silly not to take me skiing. Come along inside and we'll catch her."

Mike opened the front door cautiously. No one was in the front room, but the door to the kitchen was ajar and I could hear sounds in the other room. We moved quietly and looked into the room. Daphne Price had taken the steel box down from its cupboard shelf and placed it on the table. The top was up and she had spread the contents over the table and was examining all the papers and clippings.

I cried out indignantly. "You shouldn't be looking at those things!"

She started and turned around in dismay. When she saw who it was she tried to recover herself. "This box belongs to Mr. Oliver. It shouldn't be down here at all. I'm going to take it back to his room."

"Steven thought it would be safer here," I said. "He didn't want anyone looking into it."

"He kept it locked," Mike added.

"I can see why," Cousin Daphne said.

I couldn't tell for sure whether she had known about Alanna before she saw the contents of the box, but I had a feeling that she had, and that she was enjoying all this further evidence of what had happened when Alanna was young.

Suddenly I heard Steven's voice outside the cabin, and the deeper tones of Joe Reed. A moment later they came into the main room and crossed toward the open kitchen door. At the sight of Cousin Daphne, I had a feeling that Joe Reed meant to turn and run away. But she cried out in surprise and he stayed at Steven's side.

"You?" Cousin Daphne cried. "Where did you come from? Does Alanna know you're here?"

"Nobody knows!" For the first time that I could remember, Steven looked jubilant—happy. "Nobody knows that my father has been working up at Mr. Clausen's and pretending to be Joe Reed. I didn't know it myself until just now when I met him on the slopes."

All my notions of blackmail fell away in the face of this astonishing news. I could only stare at Joe in surprise.

"I've been waiting for a chance to see Steven," he said. "I thought I could bring him here to this cabin without anyone knowing. We could even stay here for a day, with the provisions I'd brought, and have a good visit."

Mike said, "That's wonderful, Joe. That is——" but Cousin Daphne was paying no attention to him.

"Alanna will be furious!" she burst in.

I thought of something I had to ask. "If you came down ahead of us, Steven, why weren't you here first? Why didn't we pass you?"

"You did," Steven said. "We stopped at a lookout point to see the view. It's off the trail around a rock outcropping, so we didn't see you, but you must have gone past us. Cousin Daphne, do you have to tell Mother——"

But there was no time for Daphne to answer and no time for Joe to get away, because at that moment Harry Mercer and Alanna Graham walked into the cabin. Mr. Mercer was limping a little, and Alanna was holding him by the arm.

Joe stepped behind the door as it opened, so Alanna walked past him and into the kitchen without seeing him there. The first thing she saw was the spread of clippings and papers on the table, with Cousin Daphne standing beside them. She walked to the table and picked up a clipping, as her face turned pale with shock.

"Where did you find these things?" she asked Daphne.

"I found them just now," Daphne said uneasily. "They're clippings Grandfather Burton saved from long ago."

"But you already knew about this, didn't you?" Alanna said.

Daphne began to pick up the scattered papers and thrust them back into the steel box. "No—no! I didn't know anything."

Mr. Mercer came toward the table. "What is there to know? What is going on here?" But his manner and his words were wrong. I had a feeling that he and Daphne had both known. I remembered the times I had seen them whispering together and the way they didn't want anyone else around—which meant Mike and me. The way Mr. Mercer had even tried to prevent us from coming down to the house after we had been invited.

Alanna's attention was still fixed upon the table and upon Daphne, so she had not looked around to see Joe Reed—whom I had to begin calling Mr. Nelson. But now Steven burst into the conversation.

"I think you did know, Cousin Daphne. Because you found that one picture that I kept out of the box. The one I put into an old photographic folder. And you took it away and hid it in that Greek jar. We'd never have known where it was if Jan hadn't broken the jar, so I got the picture back."

"I'm beginning to understand something," Alanna said in a low, tense voice.

Suddenly she gathered the contents of the box into her hands and dumped everything into the wood-burning stove. When she looked around for matches, Mike found some for her and helped her light them. Together they dropped one match after another in upon the yellowed, brittle paper until it flared to a blaze. And all the while Alanna talked.

"It's been you all along, hasn't it, Daphne? It's been you who've been making those telephone calls, threatening me with exposure if I didn't send money?"

"I don't know what you're talking about," Daphne began, but Alanna went right on as she placed the stove lid over the blaze.

"Oh, yes, you do. I can see it all. You happened on a little bit of information and you built it up into something wicked you could use. You—"

"*He* put me up to it!" Daphne cried. "Harry was the one who—" She broke off, realizing how much she was giving away.

Mr. Mercer began to sputter and deny, and quite suddenly Mr. Nelson, Steven's father, took charge.

"That's enough, Mercer," he said.

Alanna turned around with a little cry. "Bruce!"

He stood back, not moving toward her, his expression cool and distant. "I had to see how Steven was doing. I took a job nearby so I could watch for a chance to see him. After you'd had it fixed by court order that I wasn't to see him. I had to take this chance."

Steven broke in, facing Alanna angrily. "You're so perfect, aren't you? You're so perfect that you won't let me see my father! And yet there's all that—" He waved a hand at the crackling fire in the stove. "All the terrible things you've done!"

I found myself standing close beside Steven and I spoke to him in a low voice. "You have to let her tell you herself. You don't know anything about it. You only know how much she's changed since."

But before anyone could say anything else to him, Steven made an angry sound and ran out of the cabin. Alanna started after him, but Mr. Nelson stopped her.

"Jan is right," he said, "but let him go now. I've always thought he should have been told the story of what happened long ago. Then perhaps he'd have made up his mind in your favor, Alanna. But you were right, of course, to keep me from seeing him while I was in such bad shape." He seemed a different person from the secretive, surly man who had worked for my grandfather. His secrets were in the open now.

Alanna stared at him in surprise.

"The drug thing is over," he told her. "I've had an illness and I'm well again. I've wanted you to know, but you wouldn't talk to me on the phone, or see me. There wasn't any easy way to break down the guard you've put up against me. I've thought that through Steven—but now it's all out in the open and you have to make your own decision. Just don't keep me away from my son any longer."

Tears were bright on Alanna's cheeks and she made no effort to brush them away. "Oh, Bruce!" she said and went suddenly into his arms. But now Steven wasn't there to see.

I couldn't stare at them, so I looked at Cousin Daphne instead. She had folded herself into a chair, covering her face with her hands. Mike was watching her curiously.

"What's to become of me?" she whispered. "Oh, what is to become of me?"

Even in Bruce Nelson's arms, Alanna heard her. "Nothing will happen to you, Daphne," she told her. "You've been a wicked, foolish woman, but Grandfather Burton needs you. And you're not going to spread any word around about me, no matter how much you know. All that happened in the past is over and done with, and I've made my payment. I don't deserve to have it brought up now. As for you, Harry, you can pack your things and leave as soon as you can. If there is any spreading of rumors, I'll have you arrested for blackmail."

We didn't go back over the mountain for Alanna's car but picked up our skis to walk the short distance to the house. Mr. Nelson and Alanna walked ahead together and I knew, watching them, that they were a happy pair again. Mike and I followed them, with Daphne and Mr. Mercer straggling after us. But all the time I worried about Steven. Alanna hadn't made her peace with him yet, and he was still set against her, no matter what his father felt.

When we reached the house, Mike and I followed Alanna and Mr. Nelson—who had stopped being our Joe Reed—into the drawing room. The phone rang as we came into the room, and Alanna hesitated a moment, staring at the instrument. Then she seemed to realize that she need not be afraid of phone calls anymore, and she went toward it and lifted the receiver.

It was Gramp calling, and Alanna listened, smiling, and then thanked him and turned to us. "Your grandmother is much better and they will be home late this afternoon. So you'll be able to have Christmas together, after all."

That was wonderful news. If only the matter of Steven wasn't ending so unhappily.

"What about Steven?" I said.

Alanna looked helplessly at Mr. Nelson. "Should we search for him? I'm worried, and I wonder—"

I broke in, hurrying my words. "I think I might know where he is. Do you care if I go look for him? Maybe I could help a little before he sees you again."

She came to me, surprisingly, and kissed me on the cheek. "Dear Jan! You don't ever need to worry about not having a talent. You have the best talent of all— far better than the ability to act. It's something you do with your heart for other people."

I wasn't sure what she meant, but her words warmed me and gave me a happy feeling inside. I hurried upstairs and went directly to the room where Steven kept his mural.

As I expected, he was there. The screens were folded back and he was hard at work painting a picture in one of the first squares. I stood behind him and looked at it sadly. A young girl—Alanna—sat on a bunk bed, and on the wall above her Steven had put a window with bars.

I felt a little sick at the sight of the picture he was painting—and a little angry too. Angry because hurting Alanna—and hurting himself—was something he didn't have to do. And I told him so.

"You needn't paint a picture like that!" I cried.

He paid no attention to me. He didn't even look around.

"It's not up to you to punish her," I went on. "She's back with your father now and she's had all the punishment that was coming to her. It's time you used a little sense and let her love you the way she wants to love you. It's time to love her back."

"You don't know anything about it," Steven said, scowling again.

I could feel the tears burning my eyes. "That's not true! I can feel inside myself what you're feeling. I can feel what Alanna is feeling. It's all horrible and unnecessary and cruel. You're cruel."

He looked at me then and saw that I was crying, and his scowl went away. "I've never known anybody like you, Jan," he said, and a gentler look came over his face. "I wonder if you do know how it feels."

"I know how it ought to feel, if only you'd let it," I said. "If you and your mother and father can't be happy together now, a lot of it will be your fault. Hadn't you better think about how she'll feel when she sees that picture you've just drawn?"

He stood back and stared at the picture for a long, long moment. Then he reached out and ripped it off the wall, tore it up into little pieces, and the smile on his face was wonderful to see.

I applauded as if I were at a play and he tossed the pieces into the air.

"The mural is finished," he said. "I'll give it to her today."

"Then let's go up to see your great-grandfather," I said. "He's worried about that box and what may happen to the things in it if they fall into the wrong hands."

"All right," Steven said. "Let's go and tell him."

All the house seemed different. The movie room waited to be arranged, and I had a feeling that Alanna would have the heart for fixing it up now. The monster room was no longer that, but just the studio collection of an old man who had once been imaginative and gifted. Daphne might be crying in her room, but she would change now too. She had to. And Mr. Mercer was going away.

We walked down the hall toward Burton Oliver's room, and I felt joyful and happy inside. I wasn't going to miss the acting thing, because, like Steven, I'd been fooling myself first of all.

I knew one thing—it was going to be a beautiful Christmas.

🟡

More SIGNET Young Adult Titles You'll Enjoy

SIGNET Books You'll Enjoy

☐ **WHERE THE LILIES BLOOM by Vera and Bill Cleaver.** In the tradition of **True Grit**, a poignant, delightful novel of an irrepressible 14-year-old who vows to hold her family together, no matter what. Now a triumphant United Artists movie, introducing Julie Gholson and Harry Dean Stanton. **Where the Lilies Bloom** is the Newbery Award Honor book which the New York Times called "One of the year's most notable books."
(#Y5853—$1.25)

☐ **THE SWEET RUNNING FILLY by Pat Johnson and Barbara Van Tuyl.** A sympathetic and loving story of horses based on a real incident in the racing world.
(#T4848—75¢)

☐ **TWINK by John Neufeld.** A gutsy, sometimes real tale of a girl with cerebral palsy who could have been forgotten, and wasn't, and how love and touching and caring made the difference in the face of an almost overwhelming physical handicap. (#Q6273—95¢)

☐ **FIVE WERE MISSING by Lois Duncan.** The tense and thrilling story of five teenagers who are kidnapped from a school bus and must try to overcome their differences and work together to escape their captors.
(#Q6335—95¢)

☐ **LISA BRIGHT AND DARK by John Neufeld.** Lisa is slowly going mad but her symptoms, even an attempted suicide, fail to alert her parents or teachers to her illness. She finds compassion only from her three girlfriends who band together to provide what they call "group therapy." (#Q6275—95¢)